||||| || seven

A NOVEL BY ANTHONY BRUNO
BASED ON THE SCREENPLAY WRITTEN BY ANDREW KEVIN WALKER

St. Martin's Paperbacks

SEVEN

Copyright © 1995 by Anthony Bruno.

Cover photograph courtesy New Line Production Inc.

ISBN: 0-312-95704-1

Printed in the United States of America

St. Martin's Paperbacks edition / October 1995

10 9 8 7 6 5 4 3 2 1

ONE

Somewhere, out on the street, a car alarm started blaring—one long, relentless note that couldn't be ignored. Somerset glanced at the digital alarm clock on his nightstand. It was almost two A.M., and even though he'd been in bed for over an hour, he wasn't anywhere near sleep. He had too much to think about.

Somerset tried to block out the intrusive alarm, focusing instead on the ticking metronome he kept on his nightstand under the reading lamp. He watched the little arm swing back and forth, back and forth, tick . . . tick . . . tick . . . tick . . . .

Buying that little wooden pyramid was the best investment he'd ever made, he thought. After twenty-three years on the police force, having tried wives and girlfriends, booze and pills, shrinks and preachers, meditation and yoga, in the end this was the only thing that even vaguely calmed him down and lulled him to sleep. A simple little mechanical device. Just set it to a nice steady rhythm—like a Bach cello suite's, for example—and watch the arm move back and forth, back and forth, tick . . . tick . . . tick . . . tick . . . until his heartbeat gradually slowed down and fell into step with the metronome's call.

Somerset used the damn thing so much he was amazed it had lasted this long. It was a rare night that he didn't need it to obliterate all the crap he'd had to deal with during the day, just so he could get a few hours sleep. With twenty-three years on the force—seventeen as a homicide detective—he'd seen so much human crap, it was a miracle he could sleep at all. Only a homicide dick gets to see humanity at its absolute worst. Killings, beatings, torture, humiliation, degradation of every imaginable sort. Husbands killing wives, wives killing husbands, kids killing parents, parents beating babies to death, friends shooting friends, strangers shooting strangers. No rhyme or reason to any of it. Heat-of-the-moment things. Crimes of passion. Senseless violence. Random violence. A bullet in the head because some guy didn't like the way some other guy was looking at him. A shiv to the heart in an argument over a parking space. An arrow through the eye for cheating at Monopoly. Ten-year-olds shooting eleven-year-olds for their sneakers. Some doper jacked up on crack shooting into a crowd just because she felt like it. Somerset had come to believe that this city showed the way to the future: devolution. Society marching backwards. Homo sapiens crawling back into the muck where they came from.

Somerset closed his eyes and covered his face with his long fingers. He'd seen enough, and he didn't want to see anymore. He focused on the metronome's steady click coming out of the blackness behind his eyelids as the car alarm gradually faded to white noise. After twenty-three years it was amazing he could still do this.

If he stayed any longer, though, he might not be able to. The kind of crud he had to put up with collects in your mind, and eventually the build-up can be fatal. But as of tonight, he could still wash it away at the end of the day. At least some of it. And eventually he hoped to flush it all away, permanently forget all the shit he'd ever seen as if it had never happened. He knew there was a good chance he might not succeed, but he sure as hell intended to try. As soon as he retired. Just seven more ever-loving days to go. Seven more days and he was history in this town. Seven days to sweet release.

Somerset slid his hands off his face and stared at the bare walls of his bedroom. The pictures were down, and about half of the books in the floor-to-ceiling bookcases were packed. He'd been trying to weed through them, give some away, but it was hard for him to part with his books. One suit, one sports jacket, two pairs of pants, two ties, and seven clean shirts hung in the closet, the rest of his clothes all packed away. He scanned the bare walls. It seemed odd that these walls had seen him through two marriages. Of course, in the city, a rent-controlled apartment is worth more than a good wife. Paying alimony is cheaper than having to buy a co-op, and somehow both times he'd lucked out. They both made new lives for themselves after him, and he was happy that they did. As for child support, that was never an issue because he never wanted to have kids.

Actually at one time he did want to have kids, but not in the city. He knew what living in the city did to kids. Secretly, though, he'd always wished one of his wives would surprise him, tell him she was pregnant. It would've forced him to make some changes, maybe leave this hellhole. But as much as his first wife Michelle wanted a child, she couldn't, and Ella, his second, wouldn't, so he didn't pursue it. He put it out of his conscious thoughts, told himself that this was just the way things were going to be. Childless couples weren't that uncommon in the city. It was normal. But deep down in his heart of hearts he felt that it wasn't normal.

But forty-five wasn't too old to make a baby, he thought. He could still learn how to change a diaper at his age. It wasn't too late. He could still meet someone. Maybe. He wasn't exactly counting on it, but it was possible. Anything was possible once he got the hell out of here.

His stomach was suddenly tight. He could feel the tension in his jaw. He still wasn't totally comfortable with his decision. What if it was a big mistake? He'd lived his whole life in the city. What if he hated the country? What if it was a big bore? What if he was like a pigeon? He needed the garbage of the city to survive.

He turned his eyes toward the metronome and followed the swing arm, concentrating on the steady beat, forcing himself to stop thinking so much and relax. It was going to work out, he told himself. It was all going to work out fine if he just chilled out and let it happen. Seven more days of shit. That's all there was left. Seven days of shit and then his life started all over again. The good part, he told himself.

On the nightstand scattered around the metronome were the contents of his pockets: key ring, beat-up brown leather wallet, beat-up black leather case for his gold shield, mother-of-pearl-handled switchblade. Balanced on the edge of the nightstand was a hardcover copy of Hemingway's *For Whom the Bell Tolls*. He'd found it when he was packing and decided to re-read it. He reached over for the book and opened it to a page he'd dog-eared the first time he'd read it, almost twenty years ago. A sentence was underlined in faded pencil. "The world is a fine place, and worth fighting for."

Somerset had to laugh. That line had meant something to him twenty years ago when he was the new kid on the homicide squad. Back then the world *was* a nice place, and it *was* worth fighting for, but things had changed a lot since Hemingway was around. Obviously Papa had never imagined that the world would get this bad.

Somerset flipped the pages until he came to the piece of wallpaper that he'd stuck in there this afternoon. It was a single red rose in a square of grimy wallpaper. Somerset had discovered it at the house that afternoon during the walk-through before the closing. It was the wallpaper that was under the falling gold-flocked wallpaper in the parlor. He'd peeled away a section of the flocked paper and rubbed the old, yellowed glue off a patch of the red-rose paper with his hand, then he cut this square out with his switchblade.

Todd, the real estate agent, immediately became nervous, afraid that Somerset was going to change his mind.

"Is something wrong, Mr. Somerset?" Todd asked, fussing with the collar of his royal-blue blazer—the one with the real estate agency's insignia on the breast pocket—trying not to show that he was about to have a panic attack.

Somerset didn't answer. He kept staring at the finely etched rose, amazed at the skill of the artist, his use of deep shades of red with orangy highlights. The amount of detail in the old wallpaper genuinely surprised him. Did they really put this kind of artistry into wallpaper? Back then they did. He was willing to bet they didn't do that now, though.

"Is there something the matter, Mr. Somerset?" Todd repeated.

Somerset stuck the rose in his pocket and walked down the hall and out onto the front porch. It was a big wraparound porch, and his footsteps sounded like a funeral drum beat on the weathered boards. He scanned the neglected farmland around him and the neighbor's well-tended crops in the distance across the road. Off to the left the hills and the forest began. There wasn't a cloud in the sky, and he could almost hear the sun beaming down on him. The FOR SALE sign wobbled in a gently whistling wind.

Todd opened the squeaking screen door tentatively. "Mr. Somerset?"

Somerset went down the front steps, then turned around and stared up at the tin roof and the sun-bleached black tar squiggles where it had been patched.

"Do you have any questions, Mr. Somerset? The house does come with a one-year warranty on the furnace and all major appliances so if you're worried that—"

"No, no, that doesn't bother me. I realize the place is old. But that's not a problem. It's just that . . . it's just that everything here seems so . . . strange."

"Strange? I'm not sure I understand what you mean. I mean, I don't see anything 'strange' about this place. It needs a little fixing up, that's for sure, but—"

"No, no. I like the house. I like this whole place. I like the *idea* of this place."

SEVEN

Todd ventured a slight smile of relief. "I was just going to say, this place is about as normal as it gets."

Somerset looked off toward the forest. "That's why I want to live here. I want normal."

But by then Todd wasn't listening. He was busy pulling up the FOR SALE sign in the yard.

Tick . . . tick . . . tick . . . tick . . . Somerset glanced at the metronome, then stared down at the wallpaper rose in his hand. He missed the place already and he hadn't even moved in yet. He missed it because it seemed so unreal, so far removed from here. A ripple of panic ran through his stomach. What if he didn't make it? He was seven days away from normal, but a lot can come down in seven days. What if something happened?

He stared at the metronome and concentrated on the ticking to fight the panic. But the steady ticking reminded him of the clack of the Amtrak train he'd taken back to the city that afternoon. At first it was great to watch the farms and fields whiz by as he sat back and read Hemingway with a cigarette and a hot cup of coffee sending swirls of smoke and steam into the clear sunlight that bathed his seat. But eventually the sun became oppressive, demanding his attention as the landscape became drier and the farms turned into desert. Soon the skeletons of burnt-out cars started to litter the barren wasteland, and Somerset knew they were getting closer to the city. Factories and industrial parks appeared in the middle of nowhere, like lunar-landing colonies. Then the cookie-cutter suburbs with their unnatural lawns that had to be watered constantly to survive in the arid heat. They were lawns on life-support. Stupid. But there wasn't much about this part of the state that was very smart as far as Somerset was concerned. As the train approached the city from the north, Somerset could see layers of smog hanging over the skyline like the flattening hand of a vengeful God.

When the train arrived at the station, Somerset hadn't wanted to get out. He'd wanted to stay in his seat until it took him back to his new house. But duty called, and seven days was only a week. He could stick it out for a week, he told himself. After twenty-three years, what's another seven days?

But out on the street as he waited in line for a taxi, the reality of the city came at him full force. Cars screeching, sirens howling, people yelling, nobody caring. A crazed homeless man was in a tug-of-war with a tourist over a suitcase. "I'll get you a taxi, my man," the crazy man blathered. "I know how. I'll get you one. I'll get you the best fuckin' taxi in town." But the tourist, whose wife and two daughters hung back helplessly, didn't want the crazy man's assistance. They didn't want the crazy man to exist. Somerset was about to get involved, but he didn't have the energy. If he was going to escape this place, he couldn't be responsible for everything anymore. People had to solve their own problems. He got into the next taxi that pulled up and told the driver to take him home.

As the cab pulled away, Somerset noticed an ambulance and two squad cars, bubble lights flashing, fenders jutting out into the street. The bottleneck clogged traffic in both directions. Drivers honked their horns and cursed out their windows, annoyed with the disruption. As the cab inched closer, Somerset could see two patrolmen holding back the crowd of gawkers as two EMS workers hovered over a body sprawled out on the sidewalk. Somerset caught a glimpse of the body's bloody face and wondered why they weren't giving him oxygen if he were still alive. Somerset was tempted to get out and assist, but he stopped himself before he told the driver to stop, reminding himself that the uniforms were there and he wasn't the only homicide dick in the city. Besides, this wasn't even his precinct. Let the people in charge over here deal with it. It wasn't his job. Or at least it wouldn't be in another week.

The driver leaned on his horn when the car up ahead didn't plow through the intersection the way he wanted. "Fuck!" the driver snarled, pounding his fist on the steering wheel.

Somerset tried to catch his eye in the rearview mirror. "Don't you care?" he asked, nodding back toward the downed body on the sidewalk.

"Sure, I care," the driver snapped. "I'm fuckin' losing money standing here in traffic."

Somerset had no answer for that.

On the next block a fistfight suddenly broke out at the curb, two men in their twenties flailing away at each other. A crowd was egging them on, jeering and shouting. A squad car arrived, driving up on the sidewalk, and two patrolmen jumped out. One tried to break up the fight while the other tried to disperse the blood-thirsty crowd. Neither one was having much success.

Somerset had his hand on the door handle, about to jump out and help, but the driver suddenly gunned the taxi and sped around the rubberneckers holding up traffic, driving on the wrong side of the road.

"Crazy fucks," he spat.

When the driver finally got back into the right lane, Somerset let out a deep sigh and leaned back in his seat, closing his eyes, so he wouldn't have to see every sleazy adult-theater marquee and neon-lit porno video parlor on the strip.

"Where'd you say you were headed?" the driver asked.

Somerset opened his eyes. "Far away from here."

Yes, he thought. *Far away from here . . .*

The metronome was losing out to the car alarm, calling him back to reality. Somerset frowned at the swing arm, staring hard at it, willing it to work for him.

Tick . . . tick . . . tick . . . tick . . . tick . . . tick . . .

He closed his eyes, concentrating only on the sound of the metronome.

Tick . . . tick . . . tick . . . tick . . . tick . . . tick . . .

The car alarm faded as the metronome entered Somerset's head.

Tick . . . tick . . . tick . . . tick . . . tick . . . tick . . .

He started to breathe deeper, letting the metronome take over.

Tick . . . tick . . . tick . . . tick . . . tick . . . tick . . .

The phone rang. Somerset was jolted from a sound sleep on the first ring. He snapped his head to the side, checking the alarm clock. It was 6:19 in the morning. The metronome had wound down. The room was gray in the pre-dawn light.

"Shit . . ." Somerset groaned. *That wasn't enough sleep*, he thought as he reached for the phone. "What?" he croaked.

"Rise and shine, early bird. We got a fresh one." It was Taylor, one of the night-shift homicide dicks. "I gotta bring a vehicular to arraignment first thing, otherwise I'd do this one myself. Command said to call you. Sorry."

"Don't worry about it." Somerset reached for a pad and pen. "Where is it?"

"Fourteen-thirty-three Kennedy, Basement apartment in the front."

"Okay. I'll be there."

He threw the phone back on the cradle and tossed the covers back. His book fell on the bare floor with a thud. He stared down at it, open to the dog-eared page, the wallpaper rose standing up between the pages. He saw the line he'd underlined so long ago. "The world is a fine place, and worth fighting for."

Somerset leaned over and picked up the book. Maybe on a certain level he still did believe that the world was worth fighting for. Hell, somebody had to hold off the bad guys.

As he swung his legs out of bed, he wished he didn't care as much as he did. It would make the next seven days a lot easier.

Two

Detective Taylor, with his bushy beard, looked like a bear jammed into a black trenchcoat. He was standing there, looking through his notepad, making sure he'd given Somerset all he had, but Somerset couldn't get over the notion of a bear working homicide. He'd known Taylor for years, but this was the first time this image had ever occurred to him.

Maybe that wasn't such a ridiculous idea, he thought as he took in the crime scene. Animals dealing with animals.

The basement apartment at 1433 Kennedy Avenue was gloomy, but the bloody starburst on the living-room wall showed up just fine in the dim light. A body under a sheet on the floor was waiting to be taken out. The crime-scene photos had already been taken, but two technicians from Forensics were just getting started. Midge, the angry little brunette, was dusting for prints. Her co-workers called her Smudge behind her back.

"According to the landlady, they weren't married," Taylor said, "but they'd lived here together since December of '91. He worked on the loading dock at one of those chemical companies out in the desert. She worked nights as a toll-taker on the expressway. Taking change all night. That's enough to drive anybody batty. How much you wanna bet her lawyer doesn't use that as the basis for an insanity plea?"

Somerset hunkered down over the shotgun on the carpet next to the body.

"Don't touch that," Smudge barked. "It hasn't been dusted."

Somerset just nodded. It was too early for a fight, and with a week left to go, it wasn't worth it.

"How many shots?" he asked Taylor.

"Both barrels. The neighbors heard them."

"They hear anything else?"

"Yeah, them screaming at each other. The guy who lives in the apartment in the back said it had to have been going on for about two hours, which wasn't that unusual for these two lovebirds."

"Nobody ever complained about the noise?"

"Everybody else said you couldn't hear it upstairs unless you were really listening. The guy in the back apartment works the graveyard at the post office so he usually never heard it."

"What was he doing home tonight?"

"His day off. Or night off, I guess."

Somerset stepped over the corpse and tried to estimate where the woman was standing when she pulled the trigger. "She confess?"

"More or less. First man on the scene said she was crying too hard to really make out what she was saying. She was on the floor, trying to piece his head back together. Like Humpty-Dumpty."

Somerset stared down at the corpse and shook his

head. "Why is it always like this? It's only after the fact that they realize that the person they just blew away will cease to exist."

Taylor shrugged. "Crimes of passion. What can I tell you?"

"Yeah, right. Look at all that passion on the wall over there. A Rorschach valentine."

Taylor screwed up his face. He didn't know what Somerset was talking about, Rorschach valentine, but Smudge snapped her head up and glared at him. *Well, at least she got it,* Somerset thought. *She may be a pain in the ass, but at least she knows something about something.*

"Well, I'm outta here," Taylor said, putting his notepad away.

Somerset nodded absently. He'd was staring down at a kid's coloring book on the coffee table, a big box of Crayolas next to it. He stooped down and took out his pen to turn the pages. The coloring wasn't very good. Whoever did it had a hard time staying inside the lines.

"How many kids?" he asked Taylor.

"One. A boy. Landlady says he's six. The victim wasn't the father, though. According to the landlady."

"Did the kid see it happen?"

"I don't know." Taylor looked annoyed all of a sudden. "What the fuck kind of question is that anyway?"

Somerset kept looking through the coloring book. The kid had gone wild with a black crayon on a picture of an elephant. Somerset could imagine him holding the crayon in his little fist, pressing down with all his might.

Taylor hovered over him. "You know something, Somerset, I'm tickled fucking pink that you're finally leaving. And you know something, my friend? I'm not alone in that opinion."

Somerset ignored him and concentrated on the coloring book until Taylor suddenly snatched it up and flung it against the wall.

"Hey!" Smudge shouted. "Don't—"

"Shut the fuck up!" he shouted at her, then turned to Somerset. "What the hell is it with you? Why all these weird questions? 'Did the kid see it?' Who gives a fuck if he saw it? The DA's office ain't gonna put a kid on the stand against his own fucking mother." Taylor pointed down at the stiff on the floor. "The guy's dead, Somerset. His wife killed him. Anything else has nothing to do with anything. That's your whole fucking problem, Somerset. You wanna be everybody's shrink. You oughta put out a shingle when you retire."

Somerset stood up and looked Taylor in the eye, waiting for him to finish. The man wasn't telling him anything he didn't already know. Somerset had made more than his share of enemies over the years.

The bone-runners from the Medical Examiner's Office walked in then—a hefty black woman and a little muscle-bound Hispanic guy. Their khaki uniform shirts were tight on both of them. They'd left the gurney out in the hallway. The woman had a green body bag draped over her shoulder. "Can we take him?" the little bodybuilder asked Taylor.

"Ask him. He's in charge now."

The Hispanic guy looked to Somerset. "So? Can we take him?"

Somerset looked to Smudge. "You need the body for anything?"

"No." She didn't look up from what she was doing,

dusting a box of shotgun shells on the endtable next to the couch. If she was grateful that Somerset had had the courtesy to ask, she didn't show it.

Somerset nodded to the bone-runners, and the woman laid out the body bag on the floor while the little guy went out to get the gurney.

A young guy with a ragged, grown-out crew cut slipped into the room then. He looked like he was about thirty, and Somerset was just about to tell him to leave the premises immediately, assuming from the hip-length black leather jacket that he was some kind of reporter, but then Somerset noticed the gold shield hanging from a chain around his neck.

"Lieutenant Somerset?" he said to Taylor.

"Not me. Him." Taylor jerked his thumb at Somerset as he went out the door.

"Lieutenant, I'm David Mills." He held out his hand to Somerset. "Today's my first day on Homicide."

Smudge let out a little snort.

Lieutenant Somerset shook his hand and nodded, but didn't say anything. Mills smiled to be friendly, but the lieutenant seemed distracted and hardly paid any attention to him. Mills watched the man as he started pacing around the room. Somerset was a lean, middle-aged black man with heavy bags under his eyes and a world-weary, basset-hound face. He moved slow, but there was something about him that reminded Mills of an old tiger he'd once seen in a zoo when he was a kid. The beast didn't move much, but somehow you knew that it could rip your throat out in a heartbeat if it wanted to. Mills was still wondering why everyone at the precinct this morning had smirked or rolled their eyes when he said that the captain was going to start him out partnering with Lieutenant Somerset.

The bone-runners from the ME's office were laying out the victim in a green body bag on the floor. Somerset was busy checking out the shotgun on the floor, and Mills wasn't sure how much initiative he should take, seeing as he was a new detective and Somerset was a lieutenant.

"Never seen a green body bag," he said to the bone-runners, so that he wouldn't feel like part of the furniture. "Where I used to work, they only used black ones."

"We use all colors," the woman bone-runner answered as her partner zipped up the bag.

"Oh, yeah? I never knew they came in colors."

"Easier to keep track of 'em," the woman said. "We get a lot of bodies. Saturday nights, it's standing room only down at the morgue. Colors help."

Mills nodded as they lifted the heavy body bag onto a stainless-steel gurney. "So what's green mean?" he asked.

The woman looked at him as if he were from the moon.

"What I mean is, do the colors *mean* anything?"

"It means he's dead," Somerset said.

Mills forced a laugh, but he didn't like the sarcastic tone of Somerset's voice. He may be new to the city, but he was no lightweight, and he wanted Somerset to know that.

"I just got into town last night," Mills said, still trying to be friendly. "Things are little different here compared to my last job."

"Where was that?"

"Springfield. It's upstate."

Somerset nodded. "I know where it is. What'd you do up there?"

"I was on the homicide unit."

"How many homicides you get a year up there?"

"Oh . . . sixty, seventy, something like that."

The dwarf dusting for prints hawked up a laugh. "We get that in a month here," she said.

"Yeah, but we only had three homicide dicks up there." Mills didn't want to get into a fight ten minutes into a new job, but she had hit a nerve. The reason he'd left Springfield was because he felt it was the boondocks. The detectives up there were as slow and conservative as bankers. Mills wanted to do real police work, real investigations. He wanted to feel that he was doing something that really mattered.

"Seventy cases a year and three detectives," Somerset said as he squatted down to inspect the carpet where the body had been. "About twenty-three cases per man. Fifty weeks a year, that gives you better than two weeks per case."

"Sounds like a vacation to me," the fingerprint freak snorted.

The bone-runners snickered as they wheeled the body out the door, but the lieutenant's face didn't change.

Finally Somerset stood up and looked Mills in the eye. "Since you're just starting out here, Detective Mills, why don't we go get a coffee, so we can talk. After that, we can—"

"Actually, if it's all the same to you, I'd like to get right down to work ASAP. You don't need to waste time with any kind of transition bullshit. I mean, it's not like we're gonna have two weeks to spend on this case."

He looked at the fingerprint dwarf who was already glaring at him. Mills ignored her. "I need to start getting a feel for the city, right, Lieutenant? Meet the players, see where they hang, that kind of stuff."

Somerset just stared at him. "Can I ask you something, Detective Mills?"

"Anything, Lieutenant."

"Why here?"

"I . . . I don't follow you."

"Why come to the city? You had a good job in a nice place. Why come here?"

Mills felt that he was being put on the spot. "Well, I came here for the same reason you're here, I guess. To keep the peace, to keep the scumbags from taking over. I mean, sure, there's more opportunity for a cop down here, more room for advancement, but to be absolutely honest, I want to feel that I'm really doing some good in the world. Isn't that why you do it? Isn't that how you feel? At least wasn't that how you felt before you decided to quit?"

Somerset's eyes went cold, the tiger ready to pounce. Unconsciously Mills braced himself, but Somerset just looked at him.

"You just met me, Mills," he said evenly.

Mills pressed his lips together, his face turning red. "Maybe I'm just sick and tired of people asking me why I decided to come here? Everybody thinks I'm nuts."

"I didn't say you were nuts. It's just that I've never heard of anyone doing it this way before. Most cops want to get out of the city."

"Like you?"

Somerset's eyes turned cold again.

"Look, I thought I could do more good here. I don't know, maybe I am nuts." Mills decided to shut up because he was just making it worse, stepping in shit right off the bat. "Look, Lieutenant, it would be great if we didn't start off kicking each other in the balls. You're calling the shots here. Whichever way you want this investigation to go, you just tell me."

Somerset crossed his arms over his chest. "I'll tell you how I want this to go. I want you to look, and I want you to listen."

"With all due respect, Lieutenant, I wasn't standing around guarding the local Taco Bell up in Springfield. I worked homicide for five and a half years."

"Not here you didn't."

"I realize that, but—"

"For the next seven days, I want you to remember that. You're not in Springfield anymore." Somerset headed out the door without another word.

Mills was so pissed off he was paralyzed, his face red and his jaw clenched. The fingerprint dwarf was laughing at him. She thought this was funny. She was facing away from him, but he could see her shoulders going up and down.

Somerset called in from the hallway. "Mills."

"What?"

"You want that coffee or not?"

This time the dwarf couldn't contain herself.

At dawn the next morning, Mills was wide awake, propped up in bed with his fingers linked behind his head. He was still trying to figure out Somerset. Tracy, his wife, was asleep by his side, her blond hair splayed out over the pillow, her brow slightly furrowed. Outside the bedroom window he could hear a garbage truck churning down in the alley, momentarily drowning out the steady thrum of traffic on the boulevard. Tracy stirred with the new noise, turning over and curling into herself, putting her back to the window.

Mills studied his wife's face. There was always something about Tracy's normal expression that reminded him of an orphan—big eyes, small mouth—just a little bit pathetic, which made her that much more beautiful whenever her face spontaneously blossomed into a smile. But her expression had changed since they'd moved, and there weren't that many spontaneous smiles anymore, not that he could see. Her face was always tense. Even in her sleep she worried.

Maybe this move was a big mistake, he thought. Maybe Somerset was right. Maybe he should have stayed in Springfield.

He stared out the window at the brick wall across the alley. No, he thought, he should not have stayed in Springfield. That, he knew for sure. As for Somerset, thank God the guy was retiring at the end of the week because that was about as long as Mills thought he could take him. He was like a priest, but with a real attitude. He didn't say much, but he made his disapproval perfectly clear whenever Mills did or said something that didn't meet with his approval. And his moodiness was enough to drive anyone up a wall. Mills could see why everyone down at the precinct was so eager for him to go.

Mills looked down at the floor on his side of the bed. Mojo, their golden retriever, was gazing up at him, panting away with a hopeful doggy smile on his face, begging to be recognized. Lucky, their old collie mix, was fast asleep among the unpacked moving boxes. Mojo wasn't used to sleeping inside where he couldn't investigate every little noise he heard. Lucky was lucky; she was old and going deaf, so the city didn't bother her as much. Mills felt bad for Mojo. It was bad enough that he'd made his wife miserable, but he'd ruined his dog's life, too. He tried not to look Mojo in the eye, focusing instead on the rise and fall of Lucky's shaggy flank.

Sticking out of the box right above Lucky was his football trophy, a golden running back frozen in motion on an imitation marble pedestal. A bittersweet smile crossed Mills's face. His high-school team had won the all-state tournament his junior year. Springfield Regional had beaten a tough inner-city team with a rep for playing dirty. Mills scored one of Springfield's three touchdowns, running it in from the two-yard line on fourth down, diving over a wall of monsters all out to nail his ass.

His buddy from the neighborhood, Rick Parsons, was a senior that year. Rick had played offensive tackle. He was a big guy, built like a refrigerator with a pumpkin on top. Mean as hell on the line, but funnier than shit the rest of the time. He'd do anything to get a laugh. He never let Mills forget that it was his back Mills had used as a stepladder to make that touchdown. Mills couldn't say for sure if that was true or not—at the time there were so many bodies crunched in so tight he didn't know who was who—but it always made for a good story, especially after work at Henley's Bar and Grill when Rick would get rowdy and pull up his shirt to show the invisible cleat marks to any girl who'd look. That was how he'd met his wife, as a matter of fact.

Mills shook his head and sighed. Rick was a real character back in high school, and he only got worse with age. No one imagined he could ever be a cop, which made him perfect for undercover work. He turned out to be the best cop Springfield had ever had, no question about it. If only Mills had been there for him, the way he'd been there for Mills at the all-state tournie, Rick would still be on the force. A lump formed in Mills's throat just thinking about that rainy night, Rick out on the fire escape, Mills coming through the apartment door. If only Mills hadn't—

The phone rang, and Mojo started barking.

Tracy's head snapped up. "What is it?" she gasped.

Mills snatched the phone before it rang twice, but Mojo was spooked and he kept barking.

"Mojo, shush!" He laid his hand on Tracy's back and started to massage it. "It's okay. It's just the phone."

Her body stiffened under his hand as her eyes widened, and she stared around the unfamiliar room. "Honey . . . where are we?" she whispered in a panic.

"Home, Trace, we're home."

Mills brought the phone to his ear. "Hello?"

"Good morning." It was Somerset. "Meet me at 377 Baylor Street as soon as you can. You know where that is?"

"I'll find it." Somerset's deadpan tone instantly annoyed Mills.

"What've we got?" Mills asked.

"Possible homicide."

"What do you mean 'possible'?"

But Somerset had already hung up.

Well, fuck you, too! Mills thought angrily.

The phone bleeped loudly in Mills's hand, telling him

to hang it up, and Mojo started barking again.

"Shush, Mojo! Quiet!" Mills hissed. "You're gonna wake everybody up."

Tracy sat up. "It's all right. I'm up." She gazed around the dim room, her eyes large and childlike. She didn't look happy.

THREE

Somerset was standing in a narrow alleyway between two apartment buildings, rummaging through the trunk of his car, looking for the box of disposable latex gloves. He knew he had some—he always kept an extra box in the car. But there was just so much shit back here he couldn't find them. Officer Davis, the first uniform on the scene, stood nearby, quietly waiting for him. Davis was built like a weightlifter, big chest and small waist, arms hanging awkwardly from his broad shoulders. As Somerset continued to look for the gloves, he started to get angry. He could have sworn he had a fresh box in here somewhere. He pulled back the dark-blue rain poncho and looked under the yellow plastic box that held the breakdown kit. Nothing. Just for the hell of it he opened the yellow box, and to his surprise there it was, right beside the flares, nestled in the coiled-up jumper cables. Why the hell had he put the gloves in there? he wondered. Further proof that it was time to retire, he thought.

"Better take your flashlight, Lieutenant," Officer Davis said. "The power's out in the apartment."

Somerset went back into the breakdown kit and took

out two small high-power flashlights, the kind you can hold in your teeth while changing a flat. He shut the trunk then and scanned the garbage-strewn street, looking for Mills. *A little slow on the uptake for Mr. Gung Ho,* Somerset thought. He was a little disappointed in Mills. The way the guy had been talking yesterday, Somerset figured he'd shoot himself out a cannon to get here. Guess not.

Somerset gazed up the side of one of the brick buildings, focusing on the top-floor windows. "Anyone been inside the apartment?"

"Just me and Eric the photographer," Officer Davis said. "Nothing's been touched. Everything's the way I found it."

Mills appeared at the top of the alley then. He had a jumbo cup of coffee in one hand, a donut in the other. As he approached, Somerset could see that he looked pretty bleary.

"Morning," he mumbled as he chewed. "What do we have here?" It was a jelly donut—a messy one, too.

"Ah . . . Detective," Officer Davis said, pointing at the jelly doughnut, "I don't think you're gonna want to bring that inside."

Mills looked puzzled. "How come?"

"You'll see," Davis said. "This way." The patrolman led the way down the alley to a heavy, rusted-out door that didn't open easily, even for a weightlifter. The ungodly squeak it made when he finally shouldered his way through was worse than a fingernail on a blackboard.

The hallway inside was dim and long-neglected. Paint chips and powdered plaster from the water-damaged walls and ceiling covered the grimy tile floor. Somerset was willing to bet those chips were lead paint, too. He scowled down at the filthy floor. *Chips for tots*, he thought angrily. *Where the hell are the building inspectors? Are they all on the pad?* He shook his head as the chips crunched under his feet. *What the hell's the use?* he thought in disgust.

"Any guess as to time of death?" Somerset asked as he followed Officer Davis up the stairs, Mills bringing up the rear.

Davis shook his head. "Like I said, I didn't touch the man, but I can vouch for his face being in a plate of spaghetti for at least forty-five minutes now."

"Hold on, hold on," Mills said from the end of the line. "You mean you didn't check for vitals?"

Davis threw a weary look over his shoulder. "Do I stutter, Detective? Trust me. The man's gone. Unless he can breathe through marinara sauce."

"Jesus Christ, the way I learned it, the first thing you do in any suspected homicide is check for vitals. Or was that just something we did upstate?"

Somerset ignored Mills's sarcasm and kept walking up the steps, following the uniform as he rounded a landing and headed down a hallway to the front of the building. They stopped at an open doorway with a piece of yellow police tape stretched across it. Apartment 2A.

"Anything else you didn't do, Officer?" Mills grumbled.

Davis glared at him, muscles flexing at the corners of his jaw. "Listen, Detective, I know procedure as well as you do, but this guy was also sitting in a pile of his own shit when I walked in. If he ain't dead, I think he would've stood up and done something about himself by now. Don't you?"

Mills looked as if he wanted to say something except his mouth was full of jelly donut. Somerset decided to jump in before this got any worse. "Thank you, Officer. We'll need to talk to you again after we've looked around."

"Yes, sir. I'll be downstairs." Davis locked gazes with Mills before he headed back down the hall. Mills glared at his back over the rim of his coffee cup.

Somerset held out a flashlight to Mills. "I'm wondering, what exactly was the point of the conversation you were about to get into with Davis?"

Mills took the flashlight. "And I'm wondering how many times he's found bodies that weren't really dead until he went back to his cruiser to call it in."

"Drop it, Mills."

"For now, I will."

Somerset chose to ignore him, putting on a pair of latex gloves instead. Mills set down his coffee cup on the floor outside the door. They ducked under the tape, one after the other, and entered the dark apartment, switching on both their flashlights. An intermittent camera flash from an interior room strobe-lit the living room as they moved through it. Something on the floor in a corner caught Somerset's eye, and he swung his flashlight beam over to check it out. Next to a green plastic recycling bin, four stacks of magazines were arranged in neat bundles, tied tight with twine.

Somerset and Mills swept the room with their flashlights. A few porno magazines were on the coffee table. The couch was piled with yellowed pillows that had once been white. Two small TV sets sat on a cabinet opposite the couch.

As they went toward the room where the camera

flashes were coming from, an overpowering stench made Somerset wince. He pulled out his handkerchief and covered his nose and mouth. He flashed his light into the room and found the refrigerator. It was the kitchen. Crouched down on the floor by the sink, Eric Goodall, the police photographer, was packing up his gear. He was wearing a surgical mask and on his forehead, a small flashlight attached to an elastic headband.

Eric stood up and hoisted his camera bag over his shoulder. "Enjoy," he muttered on his way out. He wasn't one of Somerset's fans. Somerset had a habit of making people redo things whenever they did a half-assed job, and Eric Goodall specialized in half-assed jobs.

Somerset swept the room with his flashlight. It was a small kitchen. The stove was encrusted with spilled food, each burner hosting a dirty pot or pan. The counters were jammed with open jars, empty cans, discarded packaging—peanut butter, marshmallows, black olives, baked beans, frozen pizza, frozen waffles, ice cream, Pepsi. The sink was full of dirty dishes and cooking utensils. Cockroaches were feasting everywhere, unconcerned with the glare of the flashlights. The stink was incredible.

Somerset's beam followed a trail of red sauce down the front of the under-the-counter cabinets, across the filthy floor, to the chrome leg of the kitchen table. The table top was littered with dirty plates, bags of taco chips, clear plastic trays of chocolate-chip cookies, unfinished sandwiches, moldy baked potatoes encrusted with sour cream and chives, an open can of New England clam chowder, a dried-out brick of Swiss cheese, and a box of assorted donuts, most of them gone.

Mills shined his flashlight on the other end of the table. An obese man was seated there, wearing no shirt, slumped forward, face down in a plate of spaghetti, roaches nibbling at the spattered strands. It wasn't until Somerset's light joined Mills's that the man's true size became evident. He was incredibly overweight with flab draping his upper arms like water bags. Slabs of fat encased his flanks, and his gut poured out his broken zipper and hung under the table all the way down to his knees. A lone cockroach perched on the bumper of fat at the base of his neck, twitching its antennae, trying to decide where to dine next.

A long, low whistle came out of the dark. "Somebody call Guinness," Mills said. "I think we've got a record here." He moved around to the man's far side and bent down for a closer look, then squinted into Somerset's light. "Who said this was a homicide?"

"No one yet," Somerset said.

"Are we wasting our time here or what? This guy's heart has to be the size of a canned ham. If this isn't a coronary, I don't know what is."

Somerset moved closer and shined his beam down the man's enormous legs. He was barefoot, bursting out of the pants. Somerset hunkered down and pulled out a pen to lift the man's cuff. Razor wire bound the bloated ankle to the chrome chair leg. The wire was completely buried in the encrusted wound, the flesh purple and swollen above and below it.

"You want to revise your assessment, Mills?" Somerset asked.

Mills's flashlight found the man's lap. Engorged hands were tied tight with clothesline rope, wrist-to-wrist.

"Well," Mills said, "he could have tied himself up . . . to make it *look* like a murder. I saw a guy once in Springfield who wanted his family to collect on his life insurance policy. We found him with a knife in his back, figured it was a break-in gone bad. It took me a while, but I finally figured it out. He held the knife behind him with the tip between his shoulder blades, then he got up against the wall and pushed himself back into the blade—"

"Please be quiet for a while, would you?" Somerset was getting a headache.

"Excuse me. Jeez . . ."

Somerset didn't want to hear Mills's old war stories. He was trying to concentrate, trying to figure out what the hell had gone on here. He stared at the purple bruises on the man's ankles, trying to make sense of all this. How the hell did this happen? *Why* the hell did this happen?

Mills's voice came out of the dark. "Did you see this?"

"What?"

"Over here." Mills shined his light on a metal bucket under the table, crouching down to take a closer look. He leaned forward, then immediately turned his head away. "Oh, my God!"

"What is it?"

"It's puke." Mills stood up and moved as far away from the bucket as he could. "It's a bucket of goddamn puke."

"Is there any blood in it?"

"I don't know. Feel free to look for yourself. Don't let me stop you."

Somerset shined his light in Mills' face to see how he

was. He was afraid that Mills would throw up his jelly donut. Forensics would have a fit if he puked all over the crime scene. "If you feel sick, Mills, get out."

"I'm okay."

"You sure?"

"Yes, I'm sure. I've seen worse."

"In Springfield?"

Mills didn't answer.

The impatient sound of a light switch being clicked on and off filled the silence. A tall man in his fifties with a bushy moustache and thick eyeglasses was standing in the doorway. He was holding a heavy black leather case. "Wonderful," the man said, disgusted with the useless light switch. There was enough gray morning light coming through the window over the sink for Somerset to see that it was Dr. O'Neill, the medical examiner.

The doctor stepped into the kitchen without acknowledging either detective and dropped his heavy black case on the floor next to the obese man's feet. He stooped down and opened the case, which was more like a tool box than a doctor's bag. He started rummaging through it, muttering to himself. Dr. O'Neill wasn't known for his winning personality.

Somerset could see that Mills was waiting for a formal introduction, but Mills didn't know that Dr. O'Neill would probably ignore the two of them until he was ready to talk, which might not even happen. That was just the way he was. Once, a long time ago, he had confided in Somerset that he preferred dead people to living ones because they knew how to keep quiet while he was working.

Mills opened the refrigerator door, shining his flashlight inside. The refrigerator was virtually empty.

"You think it was poison?" Mills asked the doctor.

The doctor didn't answer.

Somerset opened the oven and shined his light inside. "Guessing is useless, Mills." A large roasting pan held two inches of congealed, rancid grease.

Next to the refrigerator, a beige plastic trash can was overflowing with cans and packaging. Mills was poking though it with a pen.

Dr. O'Neill was putting on a pair of latex gloves. "You girls have got Forensics waiting outside. They're chewing their tails out there. You think we'll all fit in here?"

"There's room," Mills said. "Light's the problem."

Somerset looked around the room. He could just imagine someone knocking over that bucket of puke if they all jammed in here. Two detectives weren't necessary. "Mills," he said, "go help the officers question the neighbors."

Mills bristled. "I'd like to stay on the scene, Lieutenant."

Somerset held his flashlight on the corpse as the doctor started mumbling his initial observations into a micro tape recorder. "Send one of the forensics guys in on your way out, Mills."

"But, Lieutenant—"

"Go."

Mills shined his flashlight directly into Somerset's face. Somerset squinted, but he stared into the light, waiting for Mills to do what he'd been told to do. This kid had to learn how not to take everything personally, Somerset thought. He also had to learn how not to care so much. That was the secret to survival in this job. Too bad Somerset had never learned it himself. After a long moment, Mills switched off the flashlight and stalked out of the kitchen.

Dr. O'Neill bent forward and grabbed the fat man by the jowls, lifting his face out of the spaghetti. His face was so bloated, it looked like the man may have had trouble opening his eyes wide enough to see.

"Well," O'Neill pronounced, "he is dead. That we know for sure."

"Thank you, Doctor."

"Point that light at his mouth."

Somerset leaned closer and aimed his flashlight. "What do you see?"

"Hmmm . . . See those flecks on the side of his mouth?"

"Yeah?"

"They're blue."

"So?"

"You know of any blue foods? Blueberries don't count—they're purple."

Somerset moved in closer to see what he was talking about. There were tiny blue flecks embedded in the spaghetti sauce dripping from the man's mouth. "So what is it, Doc?"

"Beats the hell out of me." He lowered the man's head back into the spaghetti.

FOUR

Mills stared through the windshield at the heavy traffic up ahead on Kennedy Avenue. Somerset was behind the wheel, a placid, almost bored look on his face. Mills hadn't said a word since they'd gotten in the car, but his stomach was roiling. He didn't like being taken for a lightweight, which was exactly what Somerset was doing. True, he was the lieutenant and Mills was the new man on the squad, but he wasn't a goddamn rookie, not by a long shot. Mills wanted Somerset to understand that, but he didn't know how to bring it up without sounding like a crybaby. But if he didn't bring it up, he was going to end up with an ulcer.

A dark brown delivery truck was double-parked up ahead, choking the flow of traffic. Mills couldn't figure out why Somerset didn't use his siren and dashboard bubble light to cut through this mess. But Somerset obviously had the patience of God because he seemed content right where he was, slowly inching ahead with all the other citizens.

"Why don't you use the siren?" Mills finally asked.

"Won't do any good."

"Why not?"

"There's no place to go. Look. It's all jammed up all the way to the boulevard."

"People down here won't pull over for a siren?"

Somerset just looked at him sideways. "Not here they don't."

Mills chewed on his bottom lip. What was that, another dig? Out in the sticks where he came from the hayseeds pulled over for police sirens. Here in the city the sophisticates didn't pay any attention to that shit. But if Mills wasn't so green, he would've known that.

Mills finally couldn't hold it in anymore. "You've seen my file, right? You've seen what I've done. Haven't you?"

Somerset shook his head, his eyes on the road. "Nope."

A sudden flush of anger colored Mills's face. Why the hell hadn't he bothered to look at his file? "Well, if you'd checked my record, you would've known that I did my time on door-to-doors. And walking the beat, too. I did that shit for a long time."

Somerset nodded, eyes still on the road. "Good."

Mills's stomach was as tight as a fist. "Lieutenant, the badge in my pocket says 'detective,' same as yours."

Somerset finally looked at him. "Mills, I made a decision. My first concern was maintaining the integrity of the crime scene. That kitchen was too small to have a bunch of bodies bumping into counters and knocking things over. That's how you lose evidence. I can't worry about whether you think you're getting enough playing time, not when there's a homicide investigation pending."

"Yeah, well, I understand that, but—" He slammed

his hand against the dashboard. "Goddamn it, just don't be jerking me off. Okay? That's all I'm asking for. Don't jerk me off."

Mills turned sideways in his seat, waiting for a response, but Somerset kept his eyes straight ahead, nodding slightly. As the silence stretched, Mills suddenly felt very foolish for blowing up like that.

"You know, Mills," Somerset finally said, "we're going to be spending a lot of time together on this case until I leave. In that time, I can show you who your friends are and I can show you who your enemies are. I can show you how to cut through the red tape. I can show you how to 'integrate,' as the captain puts it. However . . ." Somerset cleared his throat and looked at Mills sideways. "Jerking off is something you'll have to do for yourself."

It took Mills a second to realize that Somerset was kidding him.

A sly grin wrapped around Somerset's face as he glanced down at Mills's crotch. "I don't think we should have that kind of relationship, Mills. We'd start quarrelling over stupid little things."

Mills had to laugh. He couldn't believe it. Somerset actually had a sense of humor. He just shook his head. Maybe Somerset wasn't the headcase everyone made him out to be. Maybe he was all right, after all.

But then Mills looked out at the traffic jam up ahead and gritted his teeth. If only the son of a bitch would do something to get them out of this goddamn traffic, he thought.

Despite the sparkling tiles and the gleaming stainless-steel work tables, the autopsy room at the medical examiner's office smelled like a badly run pet shop. But that wasn't what was bothering Mills. It was the sight of the dead fat man who had been slit open from his chin to his crotch.

His name was Peter Eubanks, and he'd worked at a print shop downtown. His boss had last seen him the previous Thursday. He didn't show up for work on Friday, but that wasn't all that unusual for him. According to Eubanks's boss, he'd always been heavy—about two-fifty, two-sixty, five feet ten inches tall—but nothing like the way he was when he was found dead. Three hundred and four pounds. Apparently he'd gained the extra weight over the weekend. According to Dr. Santiago, some of his bones were bending from the stress.

Two stainless-steel tables had been pushed together to hold the lolling slabs of Peter Eubanks's flesh with the guts spilling out all over the place. Mills tried not to look at his face. At an autopsy the face was always the hardest thing to look at, he remembered. If you didn't focus on the face, stiffs just looked like sides of beef. It was the face that drove home the reality that this was a human being. But in this case, looking at the face was doubly disturbing because not only was the guy cut open, he was a cartoon fatso in the flesh. Even though Mills was looking right at him, it was still hard to believe that a human being could actually do this to himself.

Mills looked over his shoulder to the next table where another pathologist was working on another body. But as soon as Mills saw the tiny lifeless arm lying on the table, he realized that this was a baby, and immediately he looked at the fat man again. Babies were always the hardest to take.

Dr. Herman Santiago was standing on the other side of the fat man, his aqua-blue lab coat blotted with drying blood. He had thick black hair, well-oiled and combed into a small pompadour, and he wore thick horn-rimmed glasses. "Our friend here has been dead for a long time," the doctor said.

Somerset stood next to the doctor, nodding slowly, that same expressionless expression on his face.

Mills tried to concentrate on what the doctor was saying, but he couldn't help glancing at the face, which made him just a little bit more light-headed each time he did it. "You think it was poison, Doc?" Mills asked, forcing himself to look away from the face.

"Serology is still working on it, but I don't think so. He doesn't have the usual signs." The doctor reached into the man's belly and moved some fat out of the way. It made a loud squish. "See this?" the doctor said. He was holding some big organ; Mills had no idea which one. "In most cases this would be dark red if he had been poisoned, but as you can see, it's not. Come around this side so you can see, Detective."

Mills made a face and moved a little closer, but he still kept his distance. He could definitely do without the human sound effects.

Dr. Santiago wrinkled his nose to push his glasses up. "You okay, Detective?"

"I'm fine."

"You have seen an autopsy before, haven't you?"

"Yes, I've seen plenty of autopsies, Doc."

"You don't look well."

"I feel fine. It's just that . . ."

"It's just that what?" Somerset asked.

"It's just that . . . Well, how can somebody let himself

go the way this guy did? I mean, don't *you* find it a little disgusting?"

The doctor flashed a crooked grin. "Do you know it took four orderlies to get this guy on the table?"

"And now they all have hernias, I bet," Mills said, and he wasn't trying to be funny.

Somerset had moved over to the stainless-steel sink where a bunch of gooshy pink and yellowish blobs were arranged in piles on paper towels. He peered into the grocer's scale hanging from the ceiling. Some other bloated red organ was in there, and it weighed over twelve pounds. A line of small glass jars lined a shelf over the sink. Somerset bent his head closer and studied them intently.

Mills stared into the bloody cavity of the man's torso and shook his head, mesmerized by the sight. "How in God's name did this fat fuck ever fit through the door of his apartment?"

"Please," Somerset snapped. "It's obvious the man was a shut-in."

"Take a look at this," the doctor said. He turned over something mushy in the dead man's guts so that they could see, but Mills couldn't imagine what it was. "This is the anterior portion of the stomach," Dr. Santiago said. "See how big it is?"

Mills and Somerset hovered over the corpse. The stomach looked pretty big, but Mills didn't have a clue as to what a normal stomach should look like.

Dr. Santiago pointed along the side of the stomach where there were deep red, striated lines. "See these? They're stretch marks. Over here, too." He turned the stomach over with a loud squish. "More stretch marks. This was caused by all the food he'd consumed in the hours before death occurred."

Mills forced himself to look closer. "I'm not sure I see what you're talking about."

"Look. Here . . . and here"—another loud squish—"lines of distension across the entire stomach. And see here? The stomach was starting to rip."

Somerset frowned. "Are you saying this man ate until he burst?"

"Well, no, he didn't actually burst. Not all the way. But there was considerable internal bleeding from the overload, and there was also a hematoma on the outside." He lifted the heavy flap of gut flesh and showed them an angry red bulb on the exterior of the man's belly. It was as big as a beet. "I don't think I've ever seen a hematoma that large," the doctor said.

Mills watched Somerset take a pair of latex gloves from a box on the shelf and put them on as he went to the other end of the table where the man's head was. "So what are you saying, Doctor? This guy died from eating too much?"

"Yes. I think that's exactly how he died."

"But what about these bruises?" Somerset said, turning the corpse's head to the side. The back of the head had been shaved, revealing a cluster of dime-sized circular and semicircular bruise marks. "What do you make of them?"

"I can't say. I haven't gotten to them yet."

"Looks like the muzzle of a gun was pressed against the back of his head," Somerset said.

Dr. Santiago wrinkled his nose and took a look, then started to nod. "Very possible. If the gun was pushed hard enough against the skin, sure."

Mills went over to see for himself, getting up close to

inspect the bruise marks. "See these?" He pointed with his pinky without touching. Above some of the circles, there was a short line at the twelve-o'clock position. "Looks like these lines were made by the front sight of a pistol. We should get Ballistics in on this. See if they can get us a list of what guns have sights that're flush with the muzzle." Mills was glad that he had noticed the sight marks before they did. He'd told Somerset that he was no rookie. "Ladies and gentlemen, I think this confirms it. We definitely have a homicide here."

Somerset just looked at him, his expression vaguely disapproving.

Mills was instantly deflated. He'd expected at least a small acknowledgement from the lieutenant for his perceptiveness.

"Doctor," Somerset said, walking back to the sink, "I want to ask you about one of these samples." He picked up a clear glass vial about the size of a medicine bottle. Floating at the bottom in clear preserving fluid was a flurry of tiny blue flecks. "Were these blue things found around the victim's mouth?"

"No." Santiago picked up another similar bottle from the shelf. "These are the ones I recovered from the mouth area. The ones you're holding—the bigger pieces—I found those in with the stomach contents."

Somerset held up the bottle for Mills to see. They looked like blue plastic scrapings. Somerset shook the bottle, and they scurried around like snow in a paperweight.

"Any idea what this stuff is?" Somerset asked.

The doctor shrugged. "Haven't sent it down to the lab yet."

"Would you like to take a guess?" Somerset persisted.

"Haven't a clue. Four bodies came in this morning, so we're a little swamped here. As soon as I can get someone to analyze it, we'll get back to you."

Mills frowned at the blue flecks, trying to think of anything even vaguely edible that looked like that.

"Any ideas?" Somerset asked him.

Mills shrugged. "Maybe it's not food." He glanced down at the bloated corpse's assorted organs. "Maybe it's something food came in, some kind of packaging. I mean, it's not like this guy was a picky eater or anything."

Somerset put the bottle back on the shelf and snapped off his latex gloves. "Get back to me as soon as you find out anything about this blue stuff, will ya, Doc?" He tossed his gloves in the garbage and headed for the door without saying another word to Mills.

Mills scowled at Somerset's back. *Some partner*, he thought.

FIVE

Back at the precinct later that afternoon, the captain was sitting at his desk, staring down at the "fat man" paperwork on his desk. Peter Eubanks, the victim, had ceased to have a name; everyone on the case simply referred to him as the "fat man." Mills had to admit that even he was doing it. They'd only found the guy's body this morning, but already his identity was dead and buried. Killers, people tend to remember, but victims become old news very quickly.

Mills waited while the captain read the initial report from the ME's office. The captain was in his late forties/early fifties, with big bags under his eyes, immovable Grecian Formula hair, and a bad complexion. Mills tried not to stare at the side of the captain's face where a patch of flesh pulsated each time he clenched his jaw, which he did constantly. Mills had noticed that the captain had a habit of doing this whenever he wasn't talking.

The captain's office was bigger than everyone else's in the precinct house, but not by much. He had three windows, but a crummy view: lots of tenement buildings and urban blight. The interior walls were glass from the waist up. Closed vertical blinds blocked out the hubbub of the squad room. Mills was leaning on a low file cabinet. Somerset was sitting in one of the chairs opposite the desk, legs crossed, casually smoking a cigarette as if he were waiting for a train.

Somerset was definitely an oddball, but there was still something about him that Mills admired. For one thing, when it came to homicide, he definitely knew his shit. It had only been eight hours since the fat man had been found, but the investigation was already cooking, and that was all because Somerset had been kicking this thing in the butt all day, leaning on the right people, chewing them out when he had to, getting things done. The paperwork that was on the captain's desk right now would have taken Mills a week to assemble when he was up in Springfield.

Somerset was no diplomat, and he didn't give a flying fuck what anyone else thought of him. He'd already rubbed Mills the wrong way back at the crime scene, but that didn't matter. The guy was damn good, and Mills knew that he could learn a lot from him. Not the official, by-the-book stuff you get at the academy; Mills already knew that. It was the stuff that comes from the gut that Mills wanted, the instincts. He had a feeling Somerset had that in spades. Somerset never seemed to hesitate, not that Mills could see, and he didn't dwell on his mistakes. If he stepped on somebody's toes, so what? They'd heal. Pushing the investigation ahead was the only thing that mattered.

As Mills watched Somerset take another long drag off his cigarette, he wondered how Somerset would have reacted that night in Springfield when Rick Parsons had . . .

Mills stared out the window at the tenements across the street, his pulse suddenly racing, the memory of that night grabbing him like a seizure. It shouldn't have played out the way it did. He and Parsons had done it by the numbers, covered all their bases. It should have been a routine arrest. They each had uniform backups with them, and the description of the suspect didn't warrant unusual measures. Russell Gundersen, a forty-seven-year-old electrical engineer, who had shot his wife in a fit of despair as she was coming out of a bar one night. She'd divorced him, gotten custody of the kids, and was planning to marry a guy who lived on the East Coast. Russell was afraid he'd never see his kids again.

Russell wasn't a stone-cold killer; he was a man in pain. But even so, Mills and Parsons hadn't taken any chances. Russell lived on the top floor of a four-story walkup. Parsons went up the fire escape while Mills went to the apartment door. It was three in the morning. They were going to take him by surprise, do it by the book. At three-ten on the nose, Mills pounded on the door, just the way they'd planned it. He had identified himself as a police officer, just the way he was supposed to. When Russell didn't answer the door, he let the uniforms use the battering ram to break it down. When the door gave way, he pushed past the uniforms, first man in. The stereo was on, barely audible. It was playing a Viennese waltz. And Russell Gundersen wasn't lying in bed, pissing his pants the way a good little electrical engineer should have been.

No, Russell was up, fully clothed, standing in the

moonlight, holding a nine millimeter in both hands, sighting down the barrel at Rick Parsons, who was standing out on the fire escape and unaware that the suspect was there. "Drop the weapon!" Mills shouted, raising his own and drawing a bead on the man's back. "Drop it, Russell!"

But that was Mills's mistake. He hesitated.

He should've just shot the guy and put him down because Russell ended up shooting first, firing wild. He got off six shots before Mills and the uniforms finally brought him down. Russell only scored one hit. Rick Parsons took one in the left hip, not a fatal shot, but enough to throw him back over the railing of the fire escape. He fell four stories and hit the corner of a steel Dumpster. Irreparable spinal-cord damage.

Rick was a paraplegic now, wheelchair-bound for the rest of his life. Mills had used Rick as a step ladder to score a touchdown in the all-state tournie, and now Rick couldn't feel anything below the waist. Rick had two little boys of his own, both football players, but would never be able to show them his moves. All because Mills had hesitated, because he felt sorry for Russell Gundersen and all the shit he imagined his wife had put him through, because in his mind he thought Russell Gundersen was probably a reasonable guy who would listen to authority and surrender without a fuss. It wasn't supposed to come down that way.

But it did. And no matter what Rick and Tracy and the spin doctors in the department and at the mayor's office kept saying, it *was* Mills's fault.

Somerset wouldn't have hesitated, Mills thought. He would've just shot. He would've known in his gut to shoot. A suspect with a gun doesn't deserve the benefit of the doubt. You shoot him before he shoots someone else. You shouldn't even have to think about it. Somerset wouldn't have stopped to think about it. He had the instincts, the smarts, the mindset of a carnivore. He simply did what had to be done.

Mills had to get that mindset, too. That's why he'd come down here to work in the city. He wanted to learn from the pros, from the real cops, the guys who dealt with the worst of the worst every day of the week. Because after Rick Parsons had become paralyzed, Mills swore to God that he would never ever let himself hesitate again, that he would turn himself into the best goddamn cop there ever was. Because one Rick Parsons in a man's life was more than anyone could afford. He would never let that happen again. *Never.*

Mills's hands were shaking in the pockets of his leather jacket when he realized where he was. He sucked in his breath and blinked back his emotions, hoping neither Somerset nor the captain had noticed.

The captain was still looking down at the ME's report, shaking his head in disbelief. "Excuse the pun, but this is a little hard to swallow. Do you guys really buy it?"

Somerset nodded slowly. "The victim was given a choice. Eat or have your brains blown out. He ate his fill, then was forced to continue." He stood up and stretched. "The killer put the food in front of him and kept it coming. Took his time, too. Dr. Santiago thinks this might have gone on for twelve hours or more. The victim's throat was swollen, probably from the sheer effort of forcing all that food down, and there was definitely a point where he passed out. That's when the killer kicked him, presumably to wake him up, so he could keep eating."

"Sadistic motherfucker," Mills grumbled.

"This was premeditated in the extreme," Somerset said. "You want someone dead, you walk in and shoot him. You don't risk the time it takes to do this, not unless the act itself has some sort of meaning."

"Hold on, hold on," the captain said. "Maybe somebody had a beef with the fat boy and decided to torture him."

"We found two grocery receipts," Somerset said. "That means the killer stopped in the middle of everything and made a second trip to the supermarket. This killer definitely had an agenda."

The captain started clenching his jaw again, deep furrows forming between his brows. Mills understood how he felt. He hadn't wanted to believe it either.

Somerset broke the silence. "I think this is just the beginning."

"We don't know that," the captain snapped, glaring up at Somerset. "We've got *one* dead guy. Not three, not four. Not even two."

Somerset sat back down and cast a weary look at the captain. "Then what's the motive?"

The captain exploded. "Don't start, Somerset. All right? Don't start cooking things up before there's any reason to. You're good at that. We're spread thin as it is. I can't afford a task force now. And I sure as hell don't need a bunch of cameras up my ass every time I get in and out of my car. Do you hear what I'm saying, Somerset?"

Somerset put another cigarette between his lips. "I want to be reassigned."

Mills's eyes shot open. "Whoa, whoa! Where'd that come from?" Mills didn't want another partner. He wanted to stay with Somerset as long as he could, so he could learn from him. Of course, he couldn't come right out and say it.

The captain let out a weary sigh. "What're you talking about, Somerset? You've only got a week to go. What difference does it make?"

Somerset lit his cigarette. "This can't be my last case. It will go on and on, and I don't want to leave unfinished business when I go."

The captain pressed his lips together, doing his best to hold his temper. Obviously he'd been frustrated with Somerset many times before. "You're retiring, for chrissake. In six days you'll be out of here, gone, for good. Besides, you've left unfinished business before."

Somerset squinted against the rising smoke from the cigarette in his mouth. "Every other case was taken as close to conclusion as was humanly possible. Also, if I can speak freely . . ."

The captain rolled his eyes, exasperated. "Sure. We're all friends here."

Somerset pointed at Mills. "If you want my opinion, this shouldn't be his first assignment."

Mills shot up off the window sill. "What the hell? This isn't my first assignment, dickhead. You know that!"

Somerset ignored him. "This is too soon for him. He isn't ready for one of these."

"Hey, I'm right here. Say it to my face." Mills's temples were throbbing.

"Sit down, Mills," the captain snapped.

But Mills didn't want to sit down. He felt betrayed.

Here was the detective he wanted to learn from telling him to go take a hike, telling him he wasn't good enough to work the "fat man" case. "Captain, can we talk in private?" Mills said. "I mean, if he doesn't want to work with me, fine. It's not like I begged to work with him—"

"Sit!" the captain yelled, pointing at the window sill. Reluctantly Mills resumed his position, leaning against the sill. He glared sideways at Somerset, who met his gaze with emotionless calm.

To hell with you then, Mills thought. *Who the fuck needs you?*

The captain cracked his knuckles and sighed angrily, the jaw muscles dancing on the sides of his face. "Look," he finally said, "I don't have anyone else I can give this to, Somerset, and you know that. We're short-handed as it is, and nobody's going to swap, not with you."

Mills could feel the blood rushing to his head. "Just give the fat man to me, Captain. I can handle it."

The captain narrowed his eyes. "Come again, Mills?"

"If he wants out, then good-bye. Just give it to me."

The captain's eyes went from Mills to Somerset and back again. He seemed to be considering it. Anxiety gripped Mills's stomach. He wanted to take it on so he could prove himself, but he didn't want to lose Somerset—even if he was a goddamn son of a bitch.

The captain leaned forward in his seat and stared Somerset in the eye. "You serious about this killer? You really think he's just warming up?"

Somerset closed his eyes and nodded.

"Shit," the captain muttered. "As many times as I've wanted your gut feelings to be wrong, they seldom have been. That's why I'm leaving you on the fat man, Somerset. As insurance. Now don't go out of your way to make any more out of this than there is. Just give it your best shot in the time you have left. You hear me?"

Somerset just stared at the floor, smoke sifting out of his nostrils.

"As for you, Mills, I'm putting you on something else."

"But—"

"No buts. I'll shuffle some papers around and find you a new partner. Unless the Second Coming happens before sundown, you can count on there being a fresh homicide for you before midnight."

"But, Captain—"

"That's all. Now go."

Mills wanted to throw a chair through the window, he was so mad. This wasn't the way he'd planned it. This wasn't what he wanted at all. He wanted to stay with Somerset, but he also didn't want to be treated like a gopher. He didn't want to be a baby about it either. He wanted to show the captain that he could handle a case on his own, even a big-city case.

"You heard me, Mills. Get going," the captain ordered.

Mills chewed on his bottom lip as he headed for the door, following in the wake of Somerset's cigarette smoke. Somerset was already out the door.

SIX

The next morning a goofy-looking guy in white coveralls and a paint cap was standing outside Somerset's office door, taking his sweet time scraping Somerset's name off the glass. Somerset was sitting at his typewriter, trying to concentrate on the forms he had to fill out for the "fat man" case, but the sign painter was pissing him off, and not just because he was slow and lazy. To Somerset he was symptomatic of everything that was wrong with the world. People used to care about what they did, but now it seemed that no one cared. You do a shitty job, so what? You get paid anyway. The way the unions had deteriorated, some people didn't have to work very much at all and they still got paid. It was a bad situation. People felt that they deserved more than they really did. It made them want to do less and less for more and more. Why scrape paint for nine bucks an hour when you can sell dope and bring in a grand a week easy? And from the comfort of your own home. The worst part about it was that this kind of logic made sense.

Somerset took a drag off his cigarette and turned toward the window. His view was dominated by a billboard next door that showed a sleek black Japanese luxury car with a sharp-looking man behind the wheel, a classy-looking blonde up front next to him. Somerset figured that car cost at least thirty grand new. Guys making nine bucks an hour can only dream about cars and women like that. But society holds out these temptations, and some people can't resist. They have to have stuff like this in order to buy some self-esteem, so they do whatever they can to get it.

He took another drag and put the cigarette back in the ashtray, getting back to the four-part form scrolled up in his old manual typewriter. He typed with only two fingers, but he managed all right, banging out his description of the crime scene and the disposition of the body when he arrived. ". . . deep ligature marks around the ankles, encrusted with blood . . ." he typed.

A sharp knock on the door distracted him.

"Excuse me," the captain said to the sign painter as he opened the door and came in. "Can I talk to you for a minute?" he asked Somerset.

"Sure. Come on in."

The captain wedged his way into the small office, sidestepping the packing boxes on the floor. Half of them had Mills's name scrawled on the sides in black marker. He was going to be getting this office, but for the rest of the week they had to share it.

The captain sat on the edge of the desk, propping his foot up on one of Mills's boxes. His arms were crossed, and his jaw was working overtime. Somerset could tell that the captain was searching for a way to begin. But when the captain was finally about to start, the sign painter outside the door chose that moment to start scraping on the glass. The captain clenched his jaw even harder as he winced. It sounded like someone running his fingernails down a blackboard.

"Why don't you go get yourself a cup of coffee?" the captain yelled to him through the glass.

"What?" the sign painter said, cupping his ear.

The captain raised his voice so the man could hear. "Go take a break. We have to talk in here."

The man smiled and nodded, then quickly disappeared, glad to be able to put off work a little longer.

"Have you heard?" the captain asked.

"Heard what?"

"Eli Gould was found murdered late last night."

Somerset leaned back from the typewriter, not quite sure how he should take that news. Gould was a lawyer, after all.

"Someone broke into his office and bled him to death," the captain said. "Wrote the word 'greed' on the ceiling in his blood."

Somerset picked up his cigarette. "Greed?" He could think of plenty of worse things that could be said about Eli Gould.

"I'm letting Mills head up the investigation. I told him he'd have a case in no time. I just wish it had been a little less high-profile."

Somerset nodded, cigarette dangling between his lips as he went back to his typing. "I'm sure he'll do fine."

"Oh, of course. I'm not worried."

"Good." Somerset pecked out a few more words, waiting for the captain to get to the point. Out of the corner of his eye, he could see the captain's jaw muscles pumping away.

"What're you going to do with yourself out there in

the sticks, Somerset? Have you really thought this out?"

Somerset leaned back and looked up at him. "I'll get a job, maybe on a farm. Might work my own land eventually. There's plenty of work to do on the house. I won't get bored."

The captain started shaking his head. "Can't you feel it yet?"

"What?"

"Can't you feel that feeling in the pit of your stomach? You're not going to be a cop anymore."

"Right. That's the whole point."

"Come on, Somerset. Be real. You're not leaving. You only think you can leave."

Somerset stared the captain in the eye. "A man was walking his dog last night. He was attacked, had his wallet and watch taken. But while he was lying on the sidewalk unconscious, the animal who attacked him decided to stab him with a jackknife through both eyes. Last night just after nine, about four blocks from here."

"Yeah, I know about it. That's awful . . . awful. But we got the guy. Picked him up this morning. A crackhead."

"I can't live here. I have no understanding of this place anymore."

"Come on, it's always been like this."

"You think so?"

"Of course."

"You're wrong. Used to be that people killed other people for a reason, even if it was a stupid reason. But now . . . They just do it for the hell of it, just to see what'll happen. You know what the perp said when they asked him why he stabbed the man in the eyes?

He said he just wanted to see what would happen, see if the eyes would bleed blood or fluid or what." Somerset stared out at the man in the Japanese luxury car on the billboard. "I can't live here anymore."

The captain picked up the pile of paperwork next to the typewriter and straightened it, another one of his nervous habits. "You know how to do this kind of work. You were made for it, and I don't think you can deny that. I have a hard time picturing you with a tool belt and a fishing rod. But . . ." He shrugged. ". . . maybe I'm wrong."

Somerset shrugged, too. "To be honest, I don't see myself that way either. But I can't take living here anymore. I've seen more senseless shit in my time than any human being ought to. I know there are guys who work the streets their whole careers, but I can't do it anymore. I'll go nuts. There's got to be more to life than wading through crap."

The captain let out a deep breath. "I hear what you're saying. It's just that as big a pain as you can be, I don't want to lose you. They don't make cops like you anymore."

"You've got Mills. He'll work out."

"But he won't be you."

Not if he's smart, he won't, Somerset thought. *He should get out now while he's still young. Do something else. See the good side of life.*

The captain stood up to go, then suddenly stopped and reached into the side pocket of his suit coat. "I almost forgot. This came back from the lab for you." He pulled out a plastic evidence bag containing a sheet of paper and a small clear-glass vial.

Somerset took the bag and recognized the blue scrapings floating in the vial of clear preserving fluid.

"These were found in the fat man's stomach," the captain said.

"Yeah, I know."

"Dr. Santiago thinks they were force-fed to the man."

"Along with everything else."

"The lab says they're pieces of floor tile."

"Floor tile?"

"Yeah, you know, linoleum." The captain opened the door and let himself out.

Somerset took the bottle out of the bag and held it up to the light. He shook it and watched the blue pieces swirl around in the fluid. "Linoleum," he said to himself, trying to remember what color the floor was in Peter Eubanks's kitchen. "Linoleum."

Suddenly the sound of fingernails-on-blackboard jarred Somerset's thoughts and made his flesh crawl. He glared through the glass at the sign painter who was scraping with one hand, holding a steaming paper cup of coffee in the other.

Somerset got up and took his jacket off the back of his chair. He shrugged into the jacket and stuck the bottle in his pocket, then reached over and opened the door. "Try putting a little elbow grease into it," he muttered to the befuddled sign painter as he headed down the hall.

Standing outside the fat man's apartment, Somerset pulled out his mother-of-pearl switchblade and popped the blade. He slit the crime-scene seals on the door, then signed the roster tacked to the wall and let himself in. The place smelled of rancid food and bug spray.

Nothing in the kitchen had been touched, but Forensics decided it was okay to spray the place to keep the roaches from eating possible evidence.

He walked through the living room and stopped at the kitchen doorway. It was dead quiet, unlike the commotion that had been in here yesterday when everyone was getting on each other's nerves, trying to do his job. He stared at the empty chrome-and-vinyl chair where Peter Eubanks, the fat man, had been sitting and thought of Mills and how pissed off he'd been when Somerset had told him to leave. He wondered about Mills, wondered if he really would work out the way the captain was hoping. Mills was a little too high-strung and much too emotional for this job. Hair-trigger personalities generally don't make good cops. And it helped to be a little brain dead when you worked Homicide, at least emotionally.

Somerset pulled out a pair of latex gloves and put them on. Mills had a hell of a case to start out with— the murder of Eli Gould of all people. Gould was probably the top criminal attorney in the city. No scum was too heinous to be represented by Gould. If you could afford his retainer, he'd tap dance naked to get you off. Rumor had it that Gould had begged Jeffrey Dahmer, the cannibal serial killer, to let him represent him, offered to do it for free in exchange for exclusive book and movie rights. At least Dahmer had had the sense to tell Gould to take a hike. He wasn't that crazy.

As Somerset entered the kitchen, he thought back to one of Gould's more notorious clients, Ed Zalinski. Somerset would never forget Zalinski. The Bathing Beauty Killer was what the papers dubbed him. He was a serial killer who had murdered five young women in the county before he was caught. He got his nickname because he liked to drain his victim's blood and take a bath in it. Sick as shit. But Somerset would never forget him or the look on his face when they broke into his house and found him.

It was a ramshackle, wood-frame triple-decker on the north side. Zalinski had inherited it from his parents, so he lived by himself in the whole place. Somerset had led the arrest team, and he made sure there were uniforms covering all the exits before they went in. It was a crazy night. The city had been in a panic over the Bathing Beauty Killer, and everyone was on edge. The Homicide Squad had been working around the clock on this one, so when they had finally narrowed the list of suspects down to Ed Zalinski, they all wanted him very badly. They wanted to catch the bastard red-handed, so that a jury would have no choice but to give him the death penalty. Somerset had wanted him as badly as anyone. But as the saying goes, be careful what you wish for.

They broke down the doors, both front and back, simultaneously, unwilling to take any chances. Somerset was with the team who'd gone through the back, right on the tails of the two uniforms who'd manned the battering ram. But the house was big and sprawling, and no one responded when the uniforms yelled, "Police!"

Somerset separated from the pack and took the kitchen, sweeping the room with his weapon. No one seemed to be there, but he wasn't going to take any chances. There was a door at the far end of the kitchen. Carefully he approached it, thinking it was a walk-in pantry, thinking the sick son of a bitch could be hiding in the dark like a bat. Leading with his gun, he whipped the door open, but was surprised by what he found. It was actually a short hallway cluttered with bundles of newspapers, boxes of bottles and cans, mops and brooms and buckets that hadn't been used in years. There was an open doorway at the end of the hallway. Somerset proceeded toward it and saw that it led down to the cellar. He took the stairs slowly, one by one, crouched low, leading with his gun. A naked bulb hung from the ceiling down there, casting ominous shadows behind the furnace and water heater. At the end of the cellar near the front of the house, Somerset could see a slit of light coming from under another doorway. There appeared to be a room under the front steps.

The cement floor was gritty, and Somerset stepped cautiously, trying to be as quiet as possible as he approached the door. His heart was slamming in his chest as horrible images raced through his mind in a useless attempt to steel himself for whatever atrocity he'd find on the other side.

He positioned himself in front of the door, ready to do whatever he had to. He tried to listen for signs of activity behind the door, but all he could hear was his own blood pumping in his ears. Finally he took a deep breath and shouted, "Police!" as he kicked in the door, sweeping the room with his gun, ready to shoot at the first thing that moved.

But what he saw stunned him, dumbfounded him. The incongruity of it all was beyond instant comprehension.

It was the indignant look on Zalinski's face that made it all so weird. The man was furious that Somerset had had the nerve to invade his privacy. The fact that he was sitting in a tub full of blood from a dead German shepherd hanging from the showerhead, his face and chest smeared with gore, made no difference to him. His *privacy* had been invaded, and he was angry. Not panicked or guilty or remorseful. Indignant.

And Zalinski wore that exact same expression all throughout his trial as Eli Gould used every shyster trick in the book to convince the jury that his client was the victim of an abusive mother and therefore not responsible for his actions. And the jury bought it! They sent Zalinski to the nut house instead of to prison. Now his case goes up for review every eighteen months, and one of these days some doctor's going to declare him cured, and a judge will have no choice but to let him out. A man who feels perfectly justified taking baths in blood is going to walk the streets someday, thanks to the legal maneuverings of Eli Gould.

That was the case that put Gould on the map, and whenever Somerset heard Gould's name mentioned he immediately thought of that expression on Ed Zalinski's face and couldn't help thinking that because of Gould and lawyers like him, evil in its most grotesque forms had became acceptable.

Mills was going to have his work cut out for him on this one, Somerset thought. Eli Gould must have had plenty of enemies. Of course, with GREED smeared on the ceiling in blood, Mills couldn't overlook Ed Zalinski himself. Maybe the Bathing Beauty had snuck out of the bin to discus a little quibble he may have had with his legal bill. From what Somerset had heard, Gould did not work cheap.

"Should've stayed in Springfield," Somerset muttered as he hit the light switch in the fat man's kitchen.

This time the overhead light worked. Someone from

Forensics must've replaced the fuse.

He scanned the food-splattered counters as he went into his pocket for the little bottle containing the linoleum pieces. He looked down at the floor and compared the speckled blue linoleum with the blue fragments in the bottle. Hunkering down, he examined them up close. It seemed like a match.

He stood up again and searched the floor, looking for gouge marks. His first thought was that the victim's weight had pushed the chrome tube legs of his chair right through the plastic ends and dug into the linoleum, but the floor was unmarked under that chair. It was also unmarked under all the other chairs and under the table legs, too. He frowned and kept looking, wishing there were more light in the room. Finally he squatted down and started feeling along the edges of the cabinets, assessing every nick, scratch, and depression. But nothing he found was deep enough to match the pieces in the bottle.

Then he ran his fingers under the front of the refrigerator. Deep scratch marks formed a short arc coming out from one of the corners. Somerset studied them, then opened the bottle and fished out the two biggest pieces. He put them on the floor and tried to fit them into the gouge, turning them this way and that as if he were piecing together a puzzle. They seemed to fit, not quite perfectly, but pretty close. He put the fragments back in the jar and put the jar in his pocket. It was obvious that the floor had been damaged when someone had moved the refrigerator. He stood up and checked both sides of the refrigerator to see how closely it was wedged in, then reached back to grab an edge. It was old and heavier than he expected. He had to shift it back and forth, pulling a little on one side, then a little on the other, basically walking it out. A bead of sweat dripped down the side of his face. That's all he needed, he thought, to throw his back out a week before he had to move.

Finally he worked the refrigerator out far enough to get a look behind it. He craned his neck over the counter to see what was back there.

His eyes widened. "Sweet Jesus . . ." he murmured.

The wall was gray with dust and grime, but a large oval patch had been cleaned away. Written in grease was a single word: GLUTTONY. Taped to the wall under the word was a clean, white legal-size envelope.

The blood froze in Somerset's veins. It was like the moment he had looked into the indignant, blood-smeared face of Ed Zalinski.

He reached back for the envelope, but it was just beyond his grasp.

SEVEN

Somerset's switchblade hit the dartboard with a *thwack!* It was in the black single-score ring on the three.

He crossed his barren living room and pried it out of the cork, then went back to his position on the other side of the couch and threw it again. *Thwack!* The blade was embedded in the double-score ring on twenty, an inch above the bull's eye. He went over and pulled it out.

Except for the dartboard, the walls were empty. The built-in bookcases were mostly empty, too, the bare wood floor crowded with boxes full of books. Somerset hadn't quite finished sorting through them all. He had hundreds of books, some that he knew he'd never read again, but he was still having a hard time parting with them.

Thwack! The switchblade lodged in the triple-ring on seventeen.

The empty room reverberated with street noise coming in from the open window. Kids out in the alley were cursing like sailors, competing with a boombox that was blasting gangsta rap. Somerset knew those kids who hung out down there. Not one of them was over twelve.

He pulled out the knife and went back to his position. *Thwack!* He hit the four at the edge of the board, way off target.

He was thinking about what he'd found behind that refrigerator today. Maybe he should've kept quiet about it, he thought. He could've sat on it until the end of the week, until after he was gone. Then it wouldn't have been his headache. But it wasn't in him to do that, so now he was stuck with GLUTTONY and GREED. If he'd kept it under his hat that the murders of Eli Gould and Peter Eubanks were connected, he wouldn't have had to get involved. It wouldn't be his problem. It would be Mills's problem.

Somerset retrieved the switchblade, closed it, and set it down on the edge of the couch. Mills, he thought, sitting down on the edge and hanging his hands between his knees. He wasn't ready for this. He thought he was, but he wasn't. The kid didn't know shit. If Mills had half a brain he would've stayed in Springfield. But he wanted to be a player. He wanted the big time. Well, now he had it.

Mills had slathered like a wolf when Somerset went back to the precinct and showed him the note he'd found behind the fat man's refrigerator. Neat, block printing in ball-point pen on lined, white paper: "Long is the way, and hard, that out of hell leads up to the light."

Mills had been looking through eight-by-ten crime-scene photos from the Gould homicide when Mills walked into "their" office. The photos were all over the desk that wouldn't be his until next week. As soon as

Somerset showed him the note, he started shuffling through the pictures like a madman, looking for close-ups of the word GREED, holding them next to the note, comparing the printing. He wanted to run off and have a handwriting analysis done to make sure they were both written by the same person. It showed how wet behind the ears he was.

It was pretty obvious that this was the same person. The press hadn't gotten wind of the story yet, so it couldn't be a copycat, not yet. Worst of all, Mills was too wound up to see that the most crucial piece of evidence was staring him right in the face: the content of the note, not the handwriting. "Long is the way, and hard, that out of hell leads up to the light."

"Do you think he's trying to tell us something?" Mills asked. "Just sounds like a lot of cult crap to me."

It took a lot of self-control for Somerset to hold his tongue. But instead of telling Mills he was an idiot, he picked out one of the photos of GREED in blood and held it next to a Polaroid he'd taken of GLUTTONY in grease. "You ever hear of the seven deadly sins, Mills?"

Mills shrugged. "Yeah . . . I guess."

"Greed, gluttony, wrath, envy, sloth, pride, and lust." Comprehension gradually showed on Mills's face. "You think this guy is going to do one for each sin?"

"It seems that way, doesn't it?"

"Shit . . ." Mills was dumbfounded.

Shit, indeed, Somerset thought as he leaned back and rested his head against the arm of the couch. There were going to be five more murders if they didn't find this guy, and with Mills heading up the investigation after his retirement, Somerset had a feeling the killer would make it all the way through his list, no sweat. It wasn't that the kid was incompetent. He just didn't have any experience with this kind of shit. This was not Springfield.

Somerset glanced at his switchblade on the opposite arm of the couch. He was getting more and more pissed off the more he thought about this mess. As much as he wanted to leave this all behind, he couldn't. Not now. He couldn't just mark time till the end of the week. He *had* to get involved in this investigation.

He sat up and grabbed the switchblade, flicking the blade out. It sailed across the room and hit the board hard. *Thwack!* Triple-score ring on the seven.

Thirty minutes later, Somerset could hear thunder in the distance. He looked up at the sky to the west. Lightning flashes revealed angry-looking, purple-gray clouds in the night. The storm would be here soon, he thought. There was nothing to slow it down once it hit the desert.

As he walked along the downtown sidewalk, a cigarette between his lips, his eyes unconsciously darted between the parked cars, checking for crazies. One of the city's bigger crackhouses was in this neighborhood. Crackheads would slit your throat for the price of a rock and not even think twice about it.

A fire engine screamed by, flashing lights bouncing off the parked cars and tingeing the buildings red.

Up ahead, a businessman in a disheveled suit stood at a public phone, shouting into the receiver, then hammering it against the hook. "Fuck you, bitch! Fuck you! Fuck you!" he kept repeating, getting angrier and angrier.

Somerset passed on by, heading for the granite steps of the main branch of the public library. As he climbed the steps, he flicked his cigarette over the heads of the vagrants sleeping on the steps. It landed in the bushes.

"Spare a cigarette, man?" one of the vagrants begged. "Spare a cigarette?"

Somerset looked down into the man's grimy face. He was a young white guy, no more than thirty. Just like Mills. Somerset reached into his shirt pocket and pulled out his pack, but it was empty. "Sorry. That was my last one."

" 'S'okay, man. 'S'okay. No problem."

Somerset continued up the stairs and passed through the library's massive columns. He pounded on the glass doors with the flat of his hand. When no one answered, he pounded again, harder.

"Take it easy, take it easy. I'm coming," a muffled voice carried through the glass. A black man in his early sixties walked through the vestibule as fast as his limp would allow. It was George, the night guard.

George unlocked the door and let him in. "How you doing there?" he said with a smile.

"Okay, George. How about you?"

"Fine and dandy."

As Somerset walked across the green marble floor of the vestibule, a familiar sense of calm washed over him, easing the tension in his shoulders. He looked through the double doors beyond the check-out desk and into the library's soaring main reading room where green-shaded banker's lamps sat on long mahogany tables. Full bookshelves lined the walls from floor to ceiling. The stacks were just beyond the reading room, aisle upon aisle of more books. And there were more stacks upstairs, literally miles of books. This was paradise for Somerset. He could easily live here.

George headed up the winding marble staircase to the second floor. "Sit where you like, my friend."

"Thanks, George."

"Hey there, Smiley."

Somerset looked up to see a woolly gray head poking out over the edge of the balcony. It was Silas the custodian. Jake and Kostas, the other two security guards here, were right behind him, waving down to him.

"How's it going, gentlemen?" Somerset said.

"Not bad," Silas said, "not bad."

"Come on, George. Move that butt of yours," Kostas called down. "The cards are getting cold."

"Duty calls," George said over his shoulder to Somerset with mock weariness. "Sure you don't want to join us for a couple of hands?"

Somerset shook his head. "No thanks. I got some work to do."

"Well, make yourself comfortable. The place is yours."

Somerset grinned. "Thanks, George." He took the notepad out of his pocket and headed into the main reading room, his footsteps echoing grandly in the cathedral-like space. Pulling out a chair for himself, he switched on a lamp and started to sit down when a crack of thunder suddenly boomed through the cavernous room. A hard rain started pelting the leaded-glass skylight above.

He could hear the men upstairs talking as they played poker. "All these books," he shouted up to them, "a world of knowledge at your disposal, and you guy play poker all night."

George poked his head over the balcony and rested a boombox on the edge. "What're you talking about down there? We got culture. We got it coming out of our asses."

The other men laughed as George switched on some music. The strains of a solo piano drifted out into the open space and sifted down over the tables like a powdery snow. Somerset closed his eyes and took it in. It was a Bach fugue from *The Well-Tempered Clavier.*

Up above George was lighting a cigar with a wooden match. "You know something, Smiley, you're gonna miss us when you go. Ain't no all-night libraries out in the boonies where you're going."

"You're probably right."

"See? You *are* gonna miss us."

Somerset nodded. "Yeah . . . I just might."

George returned to his poker game, and Somerset headed for the card catalogue. He opened his notepad as he walked. On the first page he had written down the seven deadly sins and crossed out gluttony and greed.

At the card-catalogue cabinets, he searched for the *S*'s and found the drawer he wanted. Pulling it out, he brought it over to a stand-up table nearby, then found a fresh page in his notepad. *Purgatory—vol. II, Dante's The Divine Comedy*, he wrote down from memory. He didn't have to look that one up. He knew there was plenty in there about sin.

As he flipped through the cards, searching for books about the seven deadly sins, he jotted down titles and authors. If this killer had a fixation on the seven deadlies, then Somerset knew he had to know as much about them as the killer did. No, he had to know more. This person was going to kill again, Somerset had no doubt about that, but if he could figure the guy out, anticipate his thinking, maybe he could save a couple of lives at the end of his list. Maybe.

Somerset was determined to get a handle on this killer before he left. It wasn't in his nature to just leave something like this hanging. Even if they didn't catch the killer by the end of the week, which was very unlikely unless the guy turned himself in, he was going to send Mills in the right direction and help him as best he could. Mills was too stubborn to admit that he'd made a mistake in coming down to the city, but if he was set on sticking it out here, it was Somerset's obligation to show him how to get the job done right.

As the strains of the fugue mingled with the drumming of the rain on the skylight, Somerset continued to write down titles and authors. This list wasn't for him, though. It was for Mills. If Mills intended to make his mark with this case, he was going to have to do his homework, starting with Dante 101.

EIGHT

When Mills saw the crowd of reporters and the lights and the TV cameras all jammed into the lobby of Eli Gould's office building the next morning, he was tempted to pocket his shield until he got inside. He'd never seen anything like this at a crime scene before. Sure, reporters came snooping around whenever there was a homicide up in Springfield, but nothing like this mob. Of course, the DA up in Springfield generally didn't give news conferences at crime scenes, and he didn't wear Giorgio Armani suits and faggy little Italian loafers.

Mills stopped at the edge of the crowd and stared at District Attorney Martin Talbot. The man was a showboat if there ever was one—expensive suit, hand-painted silk tie, shaved head, and a gold tooth flashing from a toothpaste-commercial smile. He looked more like a pimp than a prosecutor. But it was clear that he loved the attention, and he played to the crowd like Mick Jagger to a stadium crowd. Mills was willing to bet that Talbot would be running for mayor someday. And in this crazy place, he'd probably win.

"One at a time, please. One at a time," Talbot said into the mike. "You there." He pointed to a blonde in a fire-engine red blazer, the big diamond on his pinkie outshining the ruby on his college ring.

"Mr. Talbot," the woman shouted, "can you confirm any of the rumors that Mr. Gould was forced to mutilate himself?"

Talbot flashed a little grin and shook his head. "I can't address any of the specifics while the investigation is still ongoing. You know that, Margaret."

Mills couldn't believe this guy. He was flirting at a news conference about a homicide. Unbelievable!

"You." Talbot chose a statuesque black woman holding a microphone with her TV station's call letters on a plaque glued to the front.

"Mr. Talbot, some people are saying there's a conflict of interest here with your office conducting the investigation into the death of a defense attorney who handed your prosecutors more than a few stunning defeats in court, most notably the Bathing Beauty Killer trial. Would you care to comment on that?"

Talbot flashed that little grin and cast a scolding look at her. "Selena, if that statement weren't so ridiculous, it would be offensive. There is no conflict of interest whatsoever in this investigation, and any claim that there is, or that there even could be, is patently absurd, not to mention irresponsible."

"Mr. Talbot! Mr. Talbot!" Other reporters started to shout out their questions.

"Hold on, hold on. I'm not finished. I want you all to know that I've just come from a meeting with the police commissioner, and he has assured me that his best people have been assigned to this case."

Mills's face flushed. Even though he was the primary on the Gould homicide, he knew that Talbot was talking about Somerset, not him. The whole precinct was buzzing this morning about the connection between Gould and the fat man, the Greed/Gluttony thing. Everybody was saying that Somerset couldn't retire yet, that this was right up his alley, that if this were a serial killer, Somerset was the one who could flush the guy out. No one had actually come right out and said that Mills wasn't up to the job—not that he'd heard anyway—but that was pretty much what they were implying.

"I will say right now," Talbot continued, "that this case will be the very definition of swift justice."

Swift justice, my ass, Mills thought as he worked his way through the crush, heading for the elevators.

"Detective! Detective!" The blonde in the red blazer pushed her way out of the pack to get to Mills. "Can I have a moment of your time?"

"No."

"But—"

Mills kept walking and stepped into a waiting elevator.

"Detective, I'd just like to ask you a few—"

Mills pushed the door-close button. The elevator doors shut in her face.

When he got off on the twelfth floor, the hallway was jammed with uniforms and forensic technicians coming in and out of Gould's law offices. One of Gould's partners, a man in his late fifties with badly dyed black hair, was arguing with a sergeant, demanding to know when he could have his offices back.

"Detective Mills," the sergeant called out as soon as

he spotted him, "this is Mr. Sanderson—"

"Yes, we've met," Mills said, wishing he could avoid this so he could get to work.

Sanderson immediately got in Mills's face. "Detective, this is a place of business. I have to know when—"

"We'll be out of here as soon as possible, Mr. Sanderson." Mills kept walking.

"But *when*, Detective? I need to know when."

"I don't know that yet. When I know, you'll know." Mills slipped into the office waiting room, walking briskly across the thick forest-green carpeting. The teak double doors to Gould's personal office were open.

The woman they called Smudge was up on a ladder, dusting the ceiling for prints around the word GREED. ". . . he'll fuck it up," she was saying to another technician who was on his knees, taking fiber samples from the carpet. "I mean, what can he be, twenty-nine, thirty? He doesn't know shit."

The technician on the floor suddenly noticed Mills and started clearing his throat.

Smudge looked down and cast a weary look at Mills. "Good morning, Detective." She may as well have said, "Fuck you, Detective."

"How's it coming?"

"Nothing yet," she said.

"Keep working."

"Yeah, you, too."

Mills decided to ignore that. It wasn't worth picking a fight with a bitchy dwarf. He reached into the side pocket of his jacket for his notepad and pulled out a paperback book with it. He looked down at the cover: *DANTE'S PURGATORY*. He stuck the book back in his pocket. If he was lucky, he'd lose it somewhere.

He looked over his notes as he wandered around to the back of Gould's desk and stood behind the high-back, oxblood leather chair. On the wall behind the desk, a big oil painting hung—abstract swirls in red and green and black. On top of the desk, a set of antique brass scales were positioned next to the phone. *The scales of justice*, Mills thought. *What a joke*. The brass was stained with dried blood. So was the phone. The blood on the carpet was stiff and prickly. The lettering in blood up on the ceiling had turned red-brown.

He scanned the room, trying to see the room with a fresh eye, eager to spot something everyone else had missed, so he could prove that he did know what he was doing. Maybe Somerset could find clues at the library, but the way Mills had learned it, you found evidence at the crime scene.

In the middle of the floor, a paper-tape circle had been laid down, with a four-inch line of tape in the center.

"Where's the picture?" Mills asked the technician working on the carpet.

"Over there. Against the wall."

Leaning against the baseboard on the wall opposite the desk was an eight-by-ten photograph in a gold frame inside a plastic Ziploc evidence bag. Mills went over and picked it up, studying the picture through the plastic. It was a studio shot of a middle-aged woman: false smile, too much makeup, pearls, unnatural red hair. Yesterday Gould's partner Sanderson had confirmed that it was Mrs. Gould. On the frame's glass someone—the killer, most likely—had drawn circles around her eyes in blood. They'd found the frame propped up in the middle of the floor facing the desk right where the paper-tape circle was.

The killer had set the picture down that way for a reason, he thought. But what? And why draw circles around her eyes? Was she the next target? Or did she see something? Or was there something the killer wanted them to see, something in the direction that Mrs. Gould's photo was facing? Forensics had gone through this place with a fine-tooth comb. What could they have missed? Unless it was something so big and obvious they were all overlooking it.

He stared at the desk, the phone, the brass scales, the painting, the chair, the bloody papers, the framed diplomas on the wall, the ficus tree, the bookcase, the books . . . He couldn't figure it out. What could it be? What did the killer want him to see? He looked down at Mrs. Gould's face. What was he missing?

"She your type, Detective?" Smudge was smirking down at him from up on the ladder.

"Nope. Yours?"

She wiped the smirk off. "Fuck you."

"I don't think so."

That evening Mills was slumped down in the easy chair in his living room. Unpacked boxes still took up most of the floor space, but the TV and the stereo were set up and plugged in, and both were on. A basketball game was on television, but the sound was turned down. The Sonics were losing to the Bulls in the fourth quarter. On the stereo a solo electric guitar was wailing the blues, slow and sad. He tried to concentrate on the book in his lap, but it was no use. It didn't make any sense to him.

"Fucking Dante!" He flung the book across the room. "Goddamn poetry-writing faggot!" It was the Cliff's Notes to *The Divine Comedy*.

He reached over for the mug of coffee sitting on one of the unpacked boxes and started to take a sip, then realized it was cold. He frowned and set it down on the floor, but he didn't want a hot cup badly enough to get up and fix himself one.

On top of another box, his notepad was open to the page where he'd written down the seven deadly sins: greed, gluttony, pride, envy, wrath, sloth, and lust. He glanced at the Cliff's Notes on the floor. Mojo walked over to the book, his paws clicking on the bare wood, and sniffed it for a second, then walked away.

My feelings exactly, Mills thought. A fucking waste of time, reading Dante for a homicide investigation.

· He'd read the Cliff's Notes twice and still didn't understand squat. Reading was Somerset's deal, not his. He'd never been much of a reader. But Somerset was so fucking smart, he'd probably come up with the killer at the library. DA Talbot, the captain, every cop in the precinct, even the ones who didn't like Somerset—they all thought the guy was some kind of genius, a mad scientist of criminal investigation. Well, who knows? Maybe he was. Maybe he'd bring fucking Dante in in cuffs. Yeah, maybe Dante came back from the dead and started killing people. That would be perfect for Somerset. Just his kind of thing. The papers could call him the Divine Comedy Killer. Perfect.

Mills rubbed the back of his neck. He needed some sleep, but he was too wired to sleep. Things weren't working out the way he'd planned. He'd wanted to learn from Somerset, but he didn't want to learn poetry.

He wanted to learn how to work a homicide the way they did in the city. But now he felt that he was in competition with Somerset, that they were being compared, and he just didn't measure up to the veteran. And in this town, with Somerset's rep, there was no way Mills was going to come out looking good. Not unless he brought this killer in on a leash all by himself.

Mills closed his eyes and let the sound of the blues soak into his bones. He didn't intend to give up. He was going to give this job his absolute best, but he was going to have to do it on his terms. He wasn't Somerset, and he didn't think he ever would be a Somerset.

Mills arched his neck, listening to all the little cracks and pops. Between the music and the knot between his shoulders, he didn't notice his wife Tracy standing on the threshold between the living room and their bedroom. She was watching him, worrying about him. Her face was as tense as his shoulders.

NINE

The next morning Somerset was sitting at his desk, filling out more forms on the Gluttony killing, when Mills banged through the door, weighted down with a pile of his own paperwork. His name was painted on the glass now: DET. DAVID MILLS.

Better not break it, Somerset thought to himself as the door crashed into the corner of the desk. *Could be bad luck. Like breaking a mirror.*

Mills dropped his load on the typing table in the corner, but Somerset stood and gathered up his work. "Here. Let me get out of your way."

Mills shrugged. He looked tired, too tired to argue about it. Somerset moved over to the typing table while Mills settled in at Somerset's old desk. Somerset watched him out of the corner of his eye. Mills took a thin yellow-and-black book out of the middle of his pile and shoved it into the bottom drawer. It looked like Cliff's Notes. Boning up on his Dante? Somerset wondered.

Somerset went back to the form he'd been working on, finishing off a rough diagram of the fat man's kitchen, marking off the spots were the body had been found and where the refrigerator was situated, drawing arrows where he had found the word GLUTTONY on the wall.

When he finished the form, he set it aside and looked over at Mills, who was busy sorting through dozens of crimescene photographs from the Greed murder. Somerset was tempted to go over and take a look, but he decided to stay put and mind his own business. Mills had been in a pissy mood all day yesterday, and Somerset had a feeling that Mills was beginning to resent his help. But that was okay. Mills was right to feel that way. Mills had to be his own man because in three more days Somerset was out of there, and there was no way in hell he going to come back to do consulting work. *Mills will learn*, he told himself as he went on to the next form he had to fill out. It would be trial and error for a while, but he'd learn eventually.

Of course, in this case people were probably going to die while Mills got himself sorted out. In truth, Mills really could use some help. Just to put him in the right direction. Somerset put down his pen. "This is a serial killer we're dealing with here," he said. "You do realize that."

Mills was instantly insulted, and Somerset regretted the way he'd worded that. "You really think I'm an idiot, don't you, Lieutenant?"

"No, I never said that, and I never even thought it. It's just that we haven't discussed the serial-killer aspect, and I think we should discuss it."

"I don't."

"Why not?"

"Because as soon as we start calling this guy a serial

killer, the FBI will get wind of it, and then they'll want to get involved, and it won't be ours anymore. We'll be working for them."

"But they've got the means to—"

"Forget it. I don't even want to talk about it."

"Listen, Mills, you can't do this all by—"

The phone rang then, and they both shut up. Somerset stared at it ringing on the other desk. Mills did the same.

Somerset pointed at it. "It's your phone, Mills. It's a package deal. You get the phone with the office."

Mills reached for it. "I . . . I just figured it was probably for you."

Somerset shook his head. "Not anymore."

Mills picked it up. "Mills," he said. Then he furrowed his brow and lowered his voice. "Tracy, hi. What's wrong? Is everything okay . . . ? Well, no, but you know . . . I asked you not to call me here. I'm working . . . What . . . ? Why?" Mills looked very conflicted.

"Are you sure . . . ? Why?" he said to his wife. Finally he gave in. "Okay . . . I said, okay. Hold on." He turned to Somerset. "It's my wife."

Somerset raised his eyebrows. "And?"

"She wants to talk to you."

Somerset couldn't imagine why. He got up and took the phone. "Hello?"

"Detective Somerset? I'm Tracy Mills. David's wife? I was wondering, since you two are working together, if you'd like to come over for dinner tonight."

"Well, that's . . . that's awfully nice of you . . ." Somerset had no interest in getting social with Mills and his wife. He was trying to sever all his old ties to the city, not make new ones.

"I'm a good cook," she said, trying hard to coax him. "David's told me a lot about you. I'd like to get to meet you before you leave."

"Well, I appreciate the thought, Tracy, but—"

"Please. The city hasn't been very nice to us so far. I think both David and I could use some sage advice from someone who knows the ropes." She had an irresistible laugh.

"Well . . . what are you serving?"

"The best lasagna you've ever had. What do you say?" He didn't want to, but she seemed a little desperate.

"I guess only a fool would say no. I'd be delighted to come, Tracy. Thank you very much." He hoped he wouldn't regret this.

"Is eight o'clock okay?"

"Perfect. Thank you."

"I'll see you later then," she said, sounding happier.

"Right. Bye." Somerset hung up the phone.

Mills was baffled but on the verge of belligerence. "What was that all about?"

"She invited me to dinner at your house. Tonight."

"What?"

"I'm eating at your place tonight." Somerset sat back down at the typing table.

Mills shook his head and grumbled under his breath. "Great. I wonder if *I'm* invited."

"I didn't ask," Somerset said as he started filling out a new form.

Later that evening Mills seemed uncomfortable as he and Somerset took the stairs up to his apartment. His new leather briefcase seemed out of place in his hand.

It was a businessman's hard-shell case, black and shiny. Everything else about Mills seemed utilitarian and well broken-in. They walked down the third-floor hallway in silence. A baby's cries could be heard somewhere in the building. The sounds of traffic out on the street carried in from the open stairwell windows. The hallway floor was covered with vintage black and white hexagonal tiles, pretty but as old and worn as the rest of the building. Somerset could tell that Mills wasn't keen on this dinner idea, but he wasn't exactly sure why. He suspected that resentment was only part of it.

Mills led the way to an apartment door at the front of the building and unlocked it with his key. A large dining room table took up most of the space in the cramped living room. Plates and silverware had been set for three, and two long white candles were burning in fancy crystal candlesticks. Wedding gifts, Somerset assumed.

"Hi." A young woman emerged from the kitchenette and took Somerset by surprise. He'd just assumed that Tracy Mills would be attractive—cheerleader cute actually—but he hadn't quite expected this. Tracy had a subtler kind of beauty, the kind that would fascinate a great artist. She was thin and blonde with large soulful eyes that wavered between innocent and all-knowing. Somerset felt as if her eyes were sucking him in, learning things about him automatically. "Hello, men," she said lowering her voice. Somerset let down his guard and relaxed. Her smile was absolutely lovely, like an orchid in bloom for the very first time.

Mills put down his briefcase and went over to kiss her. "Honey, I'd like you to meet Lieutenant Somerset."

Somerset smiled and shook her hand. "Hello, Tracy."

"Nice to meet you . . . in person, I mean. My husband has told me a lot about you. Except your first name."

"It's William."

"William," she repeated, savoring it like a fine wine. "William, I'd like you to meet David. David, William. I know cops like to go by their last names. Sounds tougher. But since you're both off duty, I think you can be on a first name basis tonight."

Mills forced a grin and nodded. "Whatever you say, Trace. You're the hostess."

The sounds of scratching and whining came from behind an adjoining door. "Coming," Mills called out. "I'll be right back," he said to Tracy and Somerset.

Mills opened the door, and two dogs sprang out, jumping up on his thighs, demanding his attention. He stooped down and gathered them in his arms as one licked his face and the other nuzzled his armpit. "Yes, Mojo, yes," he said. "What is it, Lucky? What?" He corralled the two dogs back into the room and shut the door behind him.

"They adore him," Tracy explained to Somerset. "If they don't get their 'quality time' as soon as he gets home, they go nuts."

Somerset nodded, staring at the closed door. He and Michelle had had a dog for a while, but eventually they'd found that it was too much of a hassle to keep one in the city. It was a nice dog, as he remembered. She was a mutt, but she looked a lot like a border collie—black and white with long silky hair. Somerset was annoyed that he couldn't remember the dog's name.

"Please, sit down, William," Tracy said. "Can I get you something to drink?"

Somerset started to take off his jacket. "I'm fine right now. Thanks." He nodded toward the kitchenette. "Smells good."

"Oh . . . thank you." She was staring at the gun in his holster. "You can put your jacket on the couch. There's not too much dog hair on it. You'll have to excuse the mess. As you can see, we're still unpacking. Excuse me a moment. I'll be right back." She disappeared into the kitchenette.

Somerset threw his jacket over the back of the couch and couldn't help noticing the desk right next to it. It was cluttered with papers and pens, opened letters, bills. What caught Somerset's eye, though, was a gold medal in its own little plastic case.

"I hear that you two were high-school sweethearts," Somerset called out, picking up the medal. "Is that really true?"

"Yes. And college, too," Tracy said through the doorway. "Pretty hokey, huh? But I knew on our first date that this was the man I was going to marry. I just knew."

"Really?"

"He was the funniest guy I'd ever met. Still is."

"*Really*?" Somerset had a hard time believing that. Mills was either brooding or raging, as far as he could tell. He took a closer look at the medal. It was a medal of valor from the Springfield Police Department.

"So you're actually an old married couple if you add up the years," Somerset called into the kitchenette.

"Yeah, I guess so," she laughed.

"Well, that kind of commitment is rare these days. Very rare."

He was putting the medal back on the desk when Tracy came back out with a steaming baking pan of lasagna. She set it down on a wrought-iron trivet on the table, looking sideways at his gun again. It clearly made her nervous, so he started to shrug out of his holster.

"I never wear it to the dinner table," he said to dispel her misgivings. "Miss Manners says it's a very gauche thing to do."

Tracy tried to laugh, but it was forced. "You know, William, no matter how often I see guns, I still can't get used to them."

"Same here." He wrapped the holster straps around the gun and stuck it in the pocket of his jacket. He took his notepad out of his shirt pocket, intending to put that in his jacket, too, but a piece of paper fell out and sailed to the floor.

Tracy bent down and picked it up for him. It was the wallpaper rose. She stared at it for a moment, then handed it back to Somerset. "What's this? Evidence?"

Suddenly self-conscious, Somerset considered making up a story, but then thought what the hell. "It's my future," he said. "It's from the old house I bought in the country. It's where I'm going to retire."

She tilted her head and looked into his face. "You have a strange way about you, William. Interesting, I mean. It's really none of my business really, but it's just nice to meet a man who . . ." She smiled down at the rose and left her thought unfinished. "If David saw that, do you know what he'd say?"

"What?"

"That you're a fag. That's how he is."

Somerset laughed. "I guess I won't be showing it to him then."

Mills came back into the room, squeezing through the doorway so that the dogs couldn't follow him in. "My babies," he said to Somerset with a shrug. "Can't live without me." The dogs scratched and cried behind the door. He went over to the stereo and turned on the CD player. The soft wail of a delta blues slide guitar filled the room; and the dogs instantly quieted down. Mills nodded toward the door. "They know I'm here when they can hear the blues."

Tracy was dishing out the lasagna at the table. "Beer or wine, William?"

He glanced at the table. A bottle of beer was already at the head of the table; a glass of red was at another setting. "Wine," he said.

As Tracy poured another glass of wine, the men took their seats, and Mills started tossing the salad. Somerset broke off a piece of garlic bread from the basket on the table and set it on the edge of his plate.

"William, why aren't you married?" Tracy asked as she took her seat.

Mills went bug-eyed. "Tracy! What the hell kind of question is that?"

"No, that's all right," Somerset said. "Actually I was married. Twice. It just didn't work out, though." He shrugged and sipped his wine.

"That surprises me," she said. "It really does."

Somerset had to laugh. "Any person who spends a significant amount of time with me soon finds that I'm . . . disagreeable. Just ask your husband."

Mills grinned sheepishly, but he couldn't disagree. "He's right about that."

"So how long have you lived here?" Tracy asked.

"Too long." He cut into his lasagna. "How do you like it here so far?"

Tracy shot a nervous glance at her husband.

"It takes time to get used to a place," Mills answered. "You know how it is."

"Sure. Of course." Somerset could see that this was a sore subject between them. "You get numb to things pretty quick, though. You'll be surprised. There are certain things in any city—"

Somerset stopped talking when he felt a violent rumbling under his feet. It quickly gained in force and volume, making the plates and silverware clatter and the dogs bark. He glanced over his shoulder, out the window. A subway train was pulling into the elevated station that ran over the avenue. He was shocked at how close it was, no more than forty feet away. Somehow he hadn't noticed it until now. Mills looked down at his plate, suddenly moody. Tracy closed her eyes and sighed.

When the train started to pull out, the plates and silverware clattered again. The dogs' barking was more frantic. Mills shouted at them through the closed door. "Lucky! Mojo! Shush!" He flashed a lame smile at his guest, trying to make it seem as if there was nothing wrong.

"It'll go away in a second," Tracy said apologetically. She was clearly dying inside. The vibrations increased as the train struggled to pick up momentum, and Somerset grabbed his wine glass before it toppled over.

The dogs whined, and something fell over in the kitchen.

Mills's forced composure rapidly deteriorated when the rumbling didn't subside fast enough. "This real estate guy—the miserable fuck—he brings us up to see this place a few times. At first, I'm thinking he's a pretty good guy, he's making time to show us the place again even though he's busy. Each time he kept hurrying us along, though. He'd only show it to us for like five minutes at a time." Mills coughed up a bitter laugh.

"Well, we found out why the first time we slept here." Tracy nodded out the window.

Somerset bit the insides of his cheeks to keep from laughing, but he couldn't hold it in. "It's sort of like one of those automatic massage chairs. A soothing, relaxing vibrating home." He laughed despite himself, pressing his thumb and forefinger to his eyes. Mills and Tracy had to laugh, too.

Somerset couldn't stop, though. "I'm sorry. I . . ."

"Oh, what the fuck," Mills said, still laughing himself. "It is funny."

Somerset took a sip of wine and straightened up. "I couldn't help but notice the medal of valor on your desk," he said to change the subject. "What was that for?"

"David took part in an arrest with—"

"Never mind about that," Mills cut her off. "He doesn't want to hear about that." Mills's mood turned surly in a flash. He clearly did not want to talk about whatever he had done to earn the medal. The fork was trembling in Tracy's hand.

Somerset tried to catch her eye, but she was looking

down at her plate. "Excuse me," she said, and abruptly left the room.

Mills dug into his food and shoveled a slab of lasagna into his mouth. He looked down at his plate as he chewed. He wouldn't look at Somerset either.

TEN

The dirty dishes were in the sink, and Tracy was in bed. The table was now covered with crime-scene photos taken at Eli Gould's office. Somerset's coffee mug sat next to Mills's beer bottle near the edge. Muddy Waters was on the stereo, but barely audible so as not to wake up Tracy. The dogs were under the table. Mojo had his chin on his paws, eyes alert to every move Mills made. Lucky was fast asleep; it was way past the old girl's bedtime. Somerset was sitting back in his chair, staring at a photo of Gould's desktop. He'd been staring at it for the past five minutes straight. Mills wondered what he was looking for, but he felt funny about asking.

Mills stood up and arched his back. He was going cross-eyed looking at all these stupid pictures. Somerset, though, was dauntless. He had the concentration of a Zen monk. Mills picked up his beer and drained it. "More coffee?" he asked just to break the quiet.

"Sure." Somerset's eyes never left the photo.

Mills picked up Somerset's mug and went into the

kitchenette, returning with a fresh cup—light and sweet, the way Somerset took it—and a cold beer for himself. Somerset was still staring at that same photo.

Mills took a swig from the bottle and rotated his head on his shoulders. "Thumb recall."

"Pardon?" Somerset said.

"They should recall thumbs as punishment for heinous crimes."

"I see." Somerset's eyes didn't waver from that photo.

Mills dropped into his chair. "Just take them back. 'Sorry, sir, but that's behavior unbefitting a higher primate. No more thumbs for you.'"

There was silence for a moment. "Thumb recall," Somerset repeated. He was still holding the photo, but he was looking at Mills now.

Mills grinned. *Made you look*, he thought. "You won't find anyone 'accidentally' selling a gun to some mook with no thumbs. No excuse if you got caught."

Somerset brought the steaming mug to his lips. "No thumbs . . . You've got a point."

"I mean, think about it. How could someone with no thumbs even pull a trigger? And driving would be tough, too. Shit, try holding a phone for any length of time without thumbs."

Somerset just stared at him. "You know, I think you're serious."

"I am." Mills's grin broke into laughter, but he really was serious. There ought to be some way to tell the predators apart from the rest of the population. In the wild, an animal's fangs usually gave him away. It was only fair that people should have the same kind of warning.

SEVEN

Somerset put down the photo and rubbed his neck. Under the table, Mojo's eyes rolled from Mills to Somerset and back again. The poor dog couldn't figure out what this stranger was doing here so late.

"Fly your scenario by me again," Somerset said, "how you think Gould was murdered. I think I'm missing something."

Mills's stomach immediately clenched. *What's wrong with it?* he thought defensively. Did Somerset think there was something wrong with his scenario?

But Mills didn't say anything. If Somerset had found a flaw in his logic, he wanted to hear it. He did want to learn from him.

"Well," Mills started, "the way I see it, our guy got into Gould's office before the building closed and security tightened up. I also think Gould must have been working late."

"I'm certain of that," Somerset said. "Gould was the busiest defense attorney in town, and he was in the middle of a trial."

Mills took another swig off his beer bottle, then continued. "His body was found Tuesday morning, okay? But get this: the office was closed all day Monday, which means that our killer could've gotten in on Friday and laid low until the cleaning crew left. He could've spent all day Saturday with Gould, all day Sunday, and maybe even Monday."

Mills picked up one of the photos from the table, a long shot of Gould's office, Gould's body propped up in the high-back leather chair. "Gould was bound and completely nude, but the killer left one arm free. He handed Gould a butcher's knife. Now see the scales on the desk. That didn't belong to Gould. It was brought in, by the killer no doubt. In one tray there was a one pound weight. In the other there was a hunk of flesh."

Somerset stared at the photo. "A pound of flesh."

Mills searched through the scattered photos until he located a photocopy of a handwritten note paperclipped to a photo of the same note showing how it had been found, pinned to the wall behind Gould's desk. "He left us a love letter. Here."

Somerset unclipped the photocopy and read it out loud. " 'One pound of flesh, no more, no less. No cartilage, no bone, but only flesh. This task done . . . and he would go free.' " Somerset frowned at the note and read it again.

"Gould's chair was soaked through with sweat and piss," Mills said. "He'd been there for quite a while."

Somerset's face was grim. "Saturday, Sunday, and Monday. The killer would want Gould to take his time, to have to sit there and think about it. Where do you make the first cut? There's a gun in your face. What part of your body is most expendable? What can you live without?"

"Gould cut along the left side of his stomach, the love handle."

Somerset picked out a half-dozen photos and cleared the rest away. He laid them out in a line as if he were setting up cards for a game of solitaire. "Look at these with fresh eyes," he said. "Don't let yourself get numb." He rearranged the photos, overlapping them so that the corpse was blocked out in three shots. "Now even though you know the corpse is there, don't think about that. Edit out the initial shock. There's always something we haven't focused on. It could be as small as lint, but it could be right in front of us and we're missing it.

Just focus until you've exhausted all the possibilities."

Mills stood over his shoulder and stared at the pictures, scanning for something he hadn't noticed before, something on the bookshelves, something in the big abstract painting on the wall, the way GREED was spelled out in blood. But no matter how hard he tried, he kept visualizing Gould's body in the pictures.

"The man is preaching," Somerset said.

"You mean punishing."

"No, preaching. The seven deadly sins were used in medieval sermons. There were the seven deadly sins and the seven cardinal virtues. They were used as a learning tool to show people how they can be distracted from true worship."

"Like in Dante?"

Somerset looked up at him. "Did you read the *Purgatorio*?"

"Yeah ... I read it. Well, parts of it. Remember the part where Dante and his buddy are climbing that big mountain, seeing all the guys who had sinned?"

"The Seven Terraces of Purgation."

"Right. But in the book, pride comes first, not gluttony. If our guy is following Dante, he isn't going in order."

"True, but for now just consider Dante as the murderer's inspiration. This is all about atonement for sin, and these murders have been like forced contrition."

"Forced what?" Mills didn't like it when Somerset used words he didn't know.

"Contrition. It's when you regret your sins, but in these two cases it wasn't because the victims loved God and genuinely wanted to repent."

"It was because someone was holding a gun to their heads."

Somerset arched his back and rolled his head. "But there were no fingerprints at either of the crime scenes."

"Nope, nothing."

"And the two victims were totally unrelated."

"As far as we know." Mills tipped the beer bottle to his lips.

"And no witnesses of any kind."

"Which I don't understand. The killer spent a lot of time with these two guys. And in the Gould murder, he had to get back out of the building. Someone should've seen him."

"Should've but didn't. Minding your own business is a science in the city. You look at someone the wrong way here, you could end up with your throat slit. I'm not surprised that a witness hasn't come forward." Somerset pulled up his chair and returned to the photos. "But I'll bet he left us another piece to his puzzle. I don't think he wants us to dead-end this soon. He wants us to follow his lead."

Mills looked at his watch. It was eleven-thirty. "Look, I appreciate being able to talk this out, but, uh—"

"This is only to satisfy my curiosity since I'm leaving at the end of the week." Somerset was staring at his line of photographs again.

"Right." Mills reached into his briefcase, which was open on a chair, and pulled out another photo. It was a picture of the framed photo of Mrs. Gould, her eyes rimmed in blood. "The missus," he said. "If the killer's telling us that she saw something, I don't know what it could be. She was out of town when it happened."

"Maybe it's a threat," Somerset suggested.

"I thought of that. We've got her in a safe house."

Another subway train rumbled into the elevated station outside, rattling the windows and making Somerset's coffee mug jump on the table. He picked it up before it spilled on the photos, but his eyes remained rivetted on the picture of Mrs. Gould. Mills kneaded the back of his neck. He wished the fucking subway would go out on strike.

As the train pulled out of the station and the noise faded away, Somerset started running his finger over the circles around Mrs. Gould's eyes. "What if it's not that she's seen something?" he said. "What if she's *supposed* to see something, but she hasn't had the chance yet?"

"Yeah, but what is it she's supposed to see?"

Somerset shrugged. "Only one way to find out."

The "safe house" was a dingy motel at the edge of town. The flood-lit sign on the road proudly proclaimed, FREE HBO IN EVERY ROOM, but when Mills and Somerset walked into Mrs. Gould's room, Mills decided that free cable was little consolation. He scanned room and tried to keep his face neutral. The walls needed painting, there was a water spot on the ceiling the size of a giant sea turtle, the double bed sagged like a hammock, and there were low-watt bulbs in all the lamps. It looked like the kind of place where a person would go to commit suicide.

Mrs. Gould was sitting on the edge of the bed, sobbing into a crumpled tissue. Her flaming red hair hadn't been attended to in days, and her face was pale and puffy from crying. She hadn't bothered with makeup either, so she looked very much like one of those troll dolls with the hair sticking up all over the place. She was wearing a fuchsia-and-forest-green jogging suit with nothing on her feet. Her toenail polish was a demure red, but her feet weren't pretty. Large veins bulged over the tops.

Other than the woman's sobs, the only other sound in the room was the intermittent bang of a rubber ball hitting the other side of the wall. The cop on duty out in the hall kept himself amused by bouncing a rubber ball against the wall. Constantly. Not only was it inconsiderate, especially at this time of night, it was driving Mills nuts, and he was about this far from going out there and shoving it down the uniform's throat.

Mills cleared his throat and tried to ignore the banging. "I'm sorry to disturb you so late, Mrs. Gould, but—"

"It's all right. I haven't slept since . . ." Her face crumpled, and she broke down into heavy sobs, covering her mouth with one hand as if she were trying to gag herself.

Mills looked to Somerset, but Somerset's face remained expressionless. They'd already decided that Mills would do the talking since he was the primary on the Gould case. "Mrs. Gould"—he opened his briefcase and pulled out the photographs—"I need you to look at a few of the photos again."

Clunk . . . clunk . . . clunk . . .

The ball. Mills grit his teeth, ready to go out there and make that asshole eat the fucking ball. "Excuse me, I'll be right back—"

"I'll take care of it," Somerset interrupted, moving toward the door. He went out into the hallway and closed the door behind him.

Mills didn't want him to go. He didn't want to be alone with the widow. He'd never liked dealing with victims' families. He cleared his throat again and held out the photos to Mrs. Gould. "I'd like you to look at these and tell me if there's anything that seems strange or out of place. Anything at all."

But she wouldn't take the photos from him. "I've looked at those a million times," she wailed. "I don't want to see them again . . . ever."

Mills pressed his lips together. He hated seeing women cry. It made him angry with himself because he never seemed to be able to do anything to make them stop. "Please, Mrs. Gould. I need you to help me if we're going to get the person who did this."

She wiped her eyes with her fingers and looked up at him, silently pleading with him to leave her alone. But as much as it pained him to be putting her through this, he knew he couldn't let up on her.

"Please, Mrs. Gould. Anything you can see that's missing or different. Anything at all."

Reluctantly she took the photos, scowling at him as she did. She flipped through them quickly, too quickly. "I don't see anything." She held them out for him to take them back.

"Take your time. Please, Mrs. Gould."

"There's nothing here," she insisted. She would not look at them again.

"Are you absolutely certain? This could be the difference between catching this guy and losing him forever. Seriously."

Somerset came back into the room. Mills hadn't even noticed that the banging had stopped.

She tried to look at the top photo, but she couldn't bring herself to do it. "I can't do this now," she cried. "*Please!*"

Mills looked to Somerset for some help with this. "Maybe we'd better wait," the older man said softly. "It can wait till tomorrow."

But Mills didn't want to wait. "There's something in these pictures that we're not seeing, Mrs. Gould. I think you're the only one who can help us with this."

"Oh, Christ!" she moaned. "All right, all right." She forced herself to look through the photos again, shuffling through them quickly.

This was useless, Mills thought.

But then she slowed down, her brow furrowing as she compared two of the shots of her husband's office taken from the same angle. They were head-on shots of his desk and chair.

"What do you see, Mrs. Gould?" he coaxed.

She pecked at top photo with a chipped red fingernail. "This painting," she said.

Mills checked the photo. Hanging on the wall behind Gould's desk was a big oil painting, at least three by four. It was an abstract painting, smears and drips in black, red, and green.

"What about the painting?" Mills asked.

She cast an accusing glance at the two of them. "Why is it hanging upside-down?"

Mills looked at Somerset who cocked one eyebrow as he looked down at the photos in the woman's hand.

Upside-down?

The moon was a small gunshot hole in the black night outside Eli Gould's twelfth-story office window. Mills hit the lights as Somerset pulled on a pair of latex gloves. "You want to do the honors?" Mills asked, nodding toward the abstract painting on the wall.

Somerset looked a little surprised. "It's *your* investigation."

"It's *your* last week on the job."

Somerset shrugged and went over to the painting, staring up at it. "You sure our people didn't move this?"

"Even if they did, those pictures were taken before the techies got to work."

Somerset grabbed the painting by the frame and lifted it off its hook. Mills was expecting another message written in blood, but except for the hook nailed into the wall, there was nothing.

"Shit," Mills grumbled. So much for his great hunch about Mrs. Gould seeing something. "I don't even want to think about all the sleep I'm missing over this."

"Hang on, hang on." Somerset leaned the painting against the side of the desk, its back facing out. "Look at this." He pointed to the eye screws in the side of the frame. There were empty screw holes just below the screws. "Maybe our guy changed the wire, so he could rehang it upside-down."

Somerset reached into his pocket for something, and Mills was more than a little surprised when he saw a pearl-handled switchblade in his hand. Somerset flicked the blade open.

Mills had to say something. "What the fuck is that?"

Somerset looked over his shoulder. "You didn't have these up in Springfield?"

"Not on cops, we didn't."

"I always believe in using what works." Somerset

carefully pierced the brown paper stapled to the back of the painting and cut along the edge to get to the hollow space behind the canvas. When he had cut along all four edges, Mills helped him pull it away. But again, there was nothing. Not on the paper or on the back of the canvas.

"Shit!" Mills said. "What a fucking waste! I should be home in bed."

But Somerset paid him no mind, turning the painting over and working his blade under the crust of the paint. He turned the blade and pried up an edge.

"Get real, Somerset. The killer didn't paint the fucking thing. Let's get the hell out of here."

Somerset made a disgusted face at the painting, realizing that Mills was probably right. "Damn it!" he said. "There must be something here that he wants us to find."

Mills shook his head. "We're screwed. He's just fucking with us."

But Somerset wasn't listening. He was doing his Sherlock Holmes thing, off in his own world, treating Mills like some nitwit Dr. Watson. Well, fuck him, Mills thought. Ol' Sherlock was on a fishing expedition now.

Somerset took a step back and stared at the space where the painting had been. He looked around the office, then moved back another step. He stopped and stared at the space again.

Mills was getting pissed. "What the fuck're you doing?"

"Quiet. I'm thinking."

Mills balled his fists, furious that Somerset was treating him like an idiot again. In a blind fury he picked up a small lamp from the credenza and was about to smash it before he got himself under control. "Motherfucker!" he grumbled, slamming the lamp back down.

Somerset reached into his pocket and pulled out a small plastic box. He opened it and took out a brush and a jar of dark dusting powder.

"You know how to do that?" Mills was skeptical, thinking they should call in Forensics to do that.

Somerset inspected the bristles of the brush. "Don't worry. I've been around for a while." He found a straight-back chair and carried it over to the wall, then stood up on it and started dusting around the hook.

"Are you serious, Somerset, or what?"

"Wait." Somerset put his face right up to the wall to study the powder residue. He took the brush and applied more powder, moving out from the hook and nail in wider strokes.

Mills tried to be patient, but he was dying to know what Mr. Know-it-all had found. "What is it? What do you see? It's nothing, right?"

"Just keep your pants on." Somerset kept working with his face to the wall until he had nearly used up his entire jar of powder. When he stepped down from the chair, Mills finally got a good look at what he had found.

The dark powder had brought it out, as clear as newsprint: HELP ME written in fingerprints.

Holy shit, Mills thought, looking at Somerset. *This fucker is Sherlock Holmes.*

ELEVEN

$\mathbf{B}$ack at the precinct, Somerset and Mills hovered over Michael Washington's back, staring at the green computer screen, waiting for something to happen. Washington, a stocky black man in his mid-forties, was the department's chief fingerprint analyst, and he wasn't happy to be working after hours. According to Somerset, he used to be a regular guy when he was just another techie in Forensics, but now he thought of himself as a nine-to-five type, too important to be roused in the middle of the night. But Somerset had to remind him that this was urgent and lives were at stake, and that his job was to serve the police, not the other way around. After about ten minutes of shouting over the phone, Somerset finally convinced Washington to drag his ass down there, but that didn't keep the man from complaining.

"I don't know what the fuck is wrong with you guys," Washington grumbled as he worked the keyboard. "If I wanted to work nights, I would've become a dick like you two boneheads. I work days. I'm not supposed to be doing this shit now. You sure this couldn't this wait till tomorrow?"

Somerset shook his head. "Not this one. I told you it's important."

"Yeah, 'important.' Go tell my wife how important it is."

Mills was just about ready to boil over, listening to all this belly-aching. "This could save lives, asshole. Just do it and shut up."

Washington glared up at him as he pushed away from the computer. "Oh, yeah? *You* fucking doing it then. I'm going back home to bed, fuckface."

"Who you calling fuckface?"

Washington stood up, knocking his chair over, ready to square off with Mills. He'd never been one to take shit from cops. Somerset got between them. "Settle down, settle down. We do appreciate you coming down here this late, Michael. Please, continue." He turned to Mills and pushed him back to the edge of the room, hissing in his face, "Be cool, will you? We need this guy."

Mills pushed Somerset's hand off his chest. "Fuck!"

Somerset shook his head and frowned. He'd worked with hotheads before, but Mills was like napalm. He wasn't going to last long if he kept this up.

They watched from a distance as Washington continued to key in codes into the computer. After a few minutes, the monitor went solid green, then the computer started to whir and click, whir and click, as enlarged fingerprint patterns appeared. The computer was comparing the prints Somerset had taken from the HELP ME message to the prints of known felons in the national crime prevention data banks.

Washington swiveled around in his chair. "I've seen this baby take as long as three days to make a match, so go cross your fingers somewhere else. I want to catch some Z's." He swiveled the chair sideways and propped his legs up on another chair, slumping down, folding his arms, and closing his eyes.

"Come on," Somerset said as he led Mills out into the hallway.

"Sweet dreams," Mills muttered on his way out.

Down the hall, there was an old blue vinyl couch. Somerset sat down on one end while Mills fed quarters into the Coke machine nearby. Somerset looked at his watch. It was twenty after one A.M.

A can of soda clunked down the chute. Mills pulled it out and popped the tab on a can of root beer, then flopped down on the other end of the couch. "You think our guy is nuts and he's crying out for help? Is that his problem?"

Somerset had to think about it for a minute. "No. I don't think so. It doesn't fit. This guy has a definite agenda. I don't think he wants to be stopped, not until he's finished."

"I don't know about that. There are plenty of freaks out there doing dirty deeds they don't really want to be doing. You know, the little voices in their heads telling them to do bad things?"

Somerset shook his head. "Not this guy. He may be hearing little voices, but he's very organized and he's driven. These weren't impulsive killings; they were extremely well-planned. He may be certifiable, but I think he's got a grand plan, and he's not going to stop until he sees it through."

An old janitor in a dark-green work uniform appeared at the end of the hallway, mopping his way around the corner.

Somerset called out to him. "How's it going, Frank?"

The janitor stopped and squinted down the hallway. "Somerset? What the fuck're you doing here?"

"Working."

"Work'll kill you, man."

"Not me. I'm retiring."

The janitor started to howl with laughter. "Yeah, right."

"It's true. This is my last week."

The man kept laughing as he continued with his mopping.

Mills sipped his soda, watching Somerset out of the corner of his eye.

"Something wrong?" Somerset asked when he noticed Mills staring.

"Can I ask you a question?"

"What?"

"Why is it that no one believes you're going to retire?"

Somerset shrugged. He didn't know how to answer that because sometimes he didn't believe it himself.

"Is it just burn-out?" Mills asked.

Somerset sighed. "What you said to Mrs. Gould tonight, about catching this guy. You meant it, didn't you?"

"Of course."

"See, I could never say something like that to her. I've seen too many of them beat the system and get off easy with insanity pleas. Or the ones who can afford it get hotshot lawyers like Eli Gould to get them off. And some of them—a lot of them—just disappear. They kill for a while, then we never hear from them again. I wish I still thought the way you do, but I can't. That's why I'm going."

"If you don't think we can get this guy, then what the hell're we doing here? You tell me."

"Picking up the pieces," Somerset said. "Taking all the evidence, all the pictures, all the samples. Writing everything down and noting what time things happened—"

"That's all? We're just record-keepers?"

"We put it all in nice neat piles, and we file it away on the slim chance that some day it'll be needed in a courtroom." Somerset rubbed his face with both hands. "Collecting diamonds on a desert island and keeping them just in case we ever get rescued. Of course, it's a pretty big ocean out there . . ."

"Bullshit. You don't believe that."

"Hey, even the most promising clues usually only lead to other clues, not convictions. So many corpses just roll away . . . unrevenged. It's sad."

Mills turned sideways and looked him in the eye. "Don't tell me that you didn't get a rush tonight, the adrenaline pumping, moving full steam ahead, really getting somewhere with this. And don't try to tell me it was only because we found something that might play well in court someday years from now."

Somerset pulled out a cigarette and took his time lighting it. Mills was right about the rush. He had gotten one, and he was going to miss that feeling. But he knew that it was always just a temporary high. A cop's best efforts rarely achieved the desired result. Ultimately it was the jury who held all the cards. Acquittals were taken as failures; pleas bargains were just sellouts.

Somerset took a long drag on his cigarette as Mills burrowed into his corner of the couch, getting comfortable. The only sounds in the precinct were the distant whir and click of the computer down the hall and the soft swoosh of the janitor's mop. He glanced sideways at Mills, who was almost asleep.

"Hey," he said.

Mills's eyes shot open. "What?"

"Shouldn't you call your wife, let her know where you are?"

Mills closed his eyes. "It's okay. She's cool."

One of the dogs was growling when Tracy suddenly woke up. She was groggy, still dressed in the clothes she'd worn for dinner, lying on top of the bed covers. She sat up and tried to focus her eyes in the dark room. She squinted at the lit numbers on digital clock on the nightstand; it was 3:41. The sounds of cars racing down the avenue outside reminded her that she wasn't in Springfield, and a heaviness fell over her as she remembered where she was and what had happened. She'd excused herself from the dinner table after dessert. The wine had gone to her head, and she just wanted to lie down for a few minutes. She must've fallen asleep.

"David?" she said, her voice sounding like a croak.

No answer. Just the insistent low growl from out in the living room.

"Mojo, shush!" she said, standing up and wandering toward the living room. She had to stop and hold onto the doorpost. She was suddenly light-headed. *Must've gotten up too fast*, she thought.

Outside a subway train rumbled into the station, rattling the apartment windows. The dirty silverware in the sink jangled against the plates. The dog growled louder.

"Mojo, be quiet!"

But when she looked under the table, she realized that it was Lucky, not Mojo, who was growling. She went over and knelt down, offered her palms to the old dog. "What is it, girl? Come."

But the dog didn't go to her, and she didn't stop growling. Lucky's eyes were on the living room windows. So were Mojo's, and even though he was quiet, the fur on his back was standing up.

"What's the matter, girl? Come."

But Lucky didn't move. Suddenly she remembered something that David had told her a long time ago. Female dogs are the best home protectors, not males. The female is the one who will raise a fuss if her home is threatened.

The subway pulled out of the station, shaking the whole apartment. Tracy froze, an uneasy feeling lodged in the pit of her stomach. She stayed down on one knee until the rumble of the train faded away. Lucky was still growling.

TWELVE

"Wake up, sleepyheads. You have a winner."

"Huh!" Mills was jolted out of a sound sleep.

Somerset was stretching and yawning. Mills clutched his head. He felt like shit. It was the next morning. They'd fallen asleep on the couch.

"I said you've got a winner. Go get the worm, early birds." It was the captain, standing over them, looking as fresh and crisp as a clean sheet of paper. Mills flipped his wrist over and looked at his watch. It was six-twenty-five A.M. *Not enough sleep*, he thought. *Not nearly enough. Never enough.*

"Here's your man." The captain dropped a photocopy into Mills's lap and handed another one to Somerset. It showed two mugshots, full face and profile, of a skinny punk with long, stringy hair and multiple earrings, head tilted back with lots of attitude. Victor Dworkin was his name, age twenty-five. He looked like trouble, but he didn't seem like a major leaguer from his stats. Of course, Russell Gundersen hadn't seemed like much either.

Somerset got up from the couch with a groan. "What's this guy's story?"

"Dworkin has a long history of mental illness," the captain said. "His parents gave him a strict Catholic upbringing, but somewhere along the line—"

"Catholic?" Mills jumped to his feet at the mention of a religion. "What else do we know about that?"

Two uniforms came clamoring down the hallway like a couple of frat boys. They were both wearing bullet-proof vests under navy-blue windbreakers with POLICE stenciled in white on the fronts and backs, both carrying riot helmets. One was holding a shotgun, the other an assault rifle. ". . . so I just told him to go fuck himself!" the one with the moustache said. The one with the buzz cut laughed like a jackass.

The captain scowled at them. "You two can shut up now!"

The two cops stopped dead in their tracks, like a couple of school kids who'd just been caught without a hall pass.

"Thank you, fuckheads," the captain said, oozing sarcasm. He stared them down until they disappeared down the corridor with their tails between their legs. "Okay,"—he turned back to Mills and Somerset—"Victor Dworkin dabbled in drugs, armed robbery, and assault. He spent a couple of months in prison for the attempted rape of a minor, but his lawyer got him out on appeal. That lawyer happened to be the recently deceased Eli Gould, Mr. Greed."

Mills's eyes lit up. He could've kissed the captain. "Yes! There's our connection."

"Hang on, Mills. As far as we can tell, Victor has also been out of circulation for a while. We have an address for him, and a search warrant's being pushed through as we speak."

A red-headed sergeant whose nickname was California came barreling down the hall, leading four more uniforms in riot gear. Mills didn't really know him except to say hello, but he seemed pretty popular with the men, and from what Mills had heard, he was the captain's right-hand man. "Have the housing cops ring the doorbell," California instructed the uniforms, "then—"

"California, listen." The captain pulled him aside. "The media swarm is going to be there within forty-five minutes. If a shot is fired, they'll be there in ten. So do it right. I want headlines, not obituaries."

Mills eyed California. The captain had obviously put him in charge of the search of Victor Dworkin's residence, and Mills was instantly jealous. In his gut he felt that he should be leading the charge, even if it was his first week on the job. The captain pulled California into a corner and continued the briefing in private.

"What do you think?" Somerset said into Mills's ear. "Does this Victor character do it for you?"

Mills thought about it for a second. "Doesn't really seem like our man, does it? I don't picture him as some punk kid."

Somerset nodded. "Me neither. Our killer seems to have more purpose. This Victor character looks like the type who has a hard time getting out of bed in the morning."

"Yeah, but what about the fingerprints?"

Somerset let out a weary sigh. "Yes, they're his . . ." He shrugged. "It must be him then."

California and the captain came out of their huddle and went over to the gang of uniforms waiting for the sergeant. Mills was getting more and more pissed, even though he knew that he had no reason to be. All he wanted was to be part of the action; he wanted to catch this guy.

He nudged Somerset. "What do you say we tag along? I want to meet Victor."

Somerset waved him off, shaking his head.

Mills grinned. "Come on. Satisfy your curiosity."

"Forget it. I'm tired."

"Come on. It may be your last chance to go out on one of these. Your last shot at getting that rush. What do you say . . . William?"

California shouted to his troops. "Shake those booties, girls. Let's roll!"

Somerset gave Mills the dirtiest look he'd ever seen.

Somerset unwrapped a fresh roll of Rolaids, popped two into his mouth, then offered the roll to Mills. Mills shook his head, both hands on the wheel of the car, eyes straight ahead. He was following California and the arrest team who were up ahead in a black, unmarked police van. It was still early, and the streets were fairly deserted, but the pristine morning light did nothing to improve the ghetto scenery.

Somerset took out his automatic and checked the clip.

Mills nodded at the weapon. "You ever take one?"

"A bullet? Never, knock wood. Thirty-four years on the job, and I've only taken my gun out three times with the intention of using it. Never fired it, though. Not once." He replaced the clip with a sharp click and put the gun back in his holster. "How about you?"

"Never took a bullet, no. Pulled my gun just once . . . and fired it."

"Oh, yeah?"

"Yup . . . It was my first time out on one of these kind of things." Mills nodded at the black van speeding toward Victor Dworkin's apartment. "I didn't think so at the time, but I was pretty wet behind the ears then." The van screeched around a corner. Mills turned the wheel and stayed right with them. "The guy had killed his wife. He was a real nerdy geek. I never expected him to be the kind who'd resist, but when we came busting through the front door of his apartment, he was holding his gun on my partner who had come up the fire escape." Mills rubbed his nose, mentally editing his story to downplay how he'd fucked up. "The guy got a shot off. I got off five."

"How did it end?"

Mills edited some more before he continued. "I got the son of a bitch. It was weird, though, when it happened. It was like it happened in slow motion."

"What happened to your partner?"

Mills's heart started to thump. "He got hit in the hip. Nothing major." He opened the window halfway and let the cool air rush over his face. He wondered if he should tell Somerset what really happened to Rick Parsons. But maybe Somerset already knew. But how would he know? Somerset said he hadn't read his file.

"Is that what you got the medal of valor for?" Somerset asked.

Mills nodded, feeling uncomfortable. "Yeah . . . basically. I had been racking up a lot of street busts at the time. I had a pretty good record."

"So how did it feel? Killing a man."

Mills sighed, editing again. "I expected it to be bad. You know, taking a human life and all that. But to be honest, I slept like a baby that night. Never gave it a second thought."

That was only because he didn't know how bad Rick's condition was until the next day. Initially the doctors thought he'd have a full recovery. But after he found out that Rick would be a paraplegic for the rest of his life, Mills didn't sleep so well. He still didn't.

Somerset held the dashboard as Mills took another sharp turn. "Hemingway wrote somewhere—I can't remember where—but he wrote that in order to live in a place like this, you have to have the ability to kill. I think he meant you truly must be able to do it, not just fake it, in order to survive."

"Sounds like he knew what he was talking about."

"I don't know. I've survived so far without killing anyone."

Mills just nodded. His heart was pounding, thinking about Rick and that night with Russell Gundersen. It was a situation just like this one. Was Victor Dworkin going to be another Gundersen? Mills wondered. Was he going to fuck up again and let Somerset take a bullet when he was just days away from retirement?

Mills gripped the wheel harder. No way, he thought. He wouldn't let that happen ever again.

Up ahead the black van veered around a police car that was blocking off the street. Two more cruisers were up on the sidewalk, flanking the entrance to a run-down tenement. The van pulled up in front of the building, and Mills stopped his car twenty feet behind them. The arrest team poured out of the back of the van, six young uniforms in vests and helmets with Plexiglas face protectors, all of them well-armed.

Somerset and Mills got out and followed them in. Mills's mouth was dry. That time with Russell Gundersen had been just like this, a split team taking an apartment, half of them through the front, the other half up the back. Mills pulled his weapon as soon as he got to the first staircase. He wished his heart would calm down.

The uniforms climbed the stairs two at a time in single file. Somerset was right behind them with Mills bringing up the rear. From the look on Somerset's face, he seemed to have it all together, but he was sweating bullets. Mills slipped past him on the next landing. The guy had one more day on the job, and Mills wasn't going to let lightning strike twice.

Mills picked up his pace to keep up with the uniforms as they headed up the stairs to the third floor. Crack vials and hypodermic needles crunched under their feet on the dilapidated stairway.

On the third floor, an old drunk in a tattered pinstripe suit was lying on the floor, eyes glazed, unable to move his head more than a few inches off the ground. They stepped over him, moving toward their objective, Victor Dworkin's apartment, number 303.

A bleached blonde in an oversized Disney World T-shirt and fuzzy slippers poked her head out the door of her apartment. California waved her off, and one sight of the troops sent her scurrying back inside. The search warrant was taped to the front of California's bulletproof vest. He silently motioned for his men to come forward with the battering ram. Mills tried to muscle his way to the front, but a burly black cop got in his way. "Sorry, detective," he whispered. "Cops before dicks."

Mills wanted to tell him to go fuck himself, that he *had* to go in first, just in case, but Somerset laid a hand on his shoulder. "Department policy," Somerset said.

California waved everyone back to make room for the two men swinging the battering ram. Mills could feel the sweat dripping down his back. *Come on! Let's go,* he thought. *Let's go!*

California glanced back to make sure everyone was ready, then he nodded once.

"Police!" he shouted, pounding on the door. "Open up! Police!" He moved out of the way. "Fuck it! Go!" he ordered.

The heavy steel battering ram splintered the door on its first shot. The second blow smashed the lock. "Move!" California ordered as he pushed past his men and shouldered the broken door open, his nine milli-meter pointed at the ceiling. "Police!" he shouted again. "Police officers!"

The other uniforms barged in, but for Mills they were slow as shit. He wanted in.

When he finally did get inside, he quickly scanned the dusty living room, looking for a place where there wasn't a uniform, hoping to find Victor Dworkin him-self, but the apartment was small, and California's men had it covered. The uniforms shouted, "Police! Police!" as they swept each room, looking for Victor. Mills hap-pened to notice that the TV set was on the floor in a corner next to the couch, and it was thick with dust.

"In here!" California shouted.

Mills moved fast, beating the other uniforms to the bedroom. A body was lying on a single bed that was against the far wall. Mills couldn't see much of the per-son because California was in the way, moving forward cautiously with both hands on his gun. He kept it leveled on the sheet-covered figure. Mills had both hands on his gun, too. All he could think of was Victor pulling out a piece from under the sheet and doing a Russell Gundersen on California.

The other uniforms arrived, pushing Mills farther into the room as they squeezed in. The black cop slipped in next to California, taking the foot of the bed while California took the head.

"Good morning, sweetheart!" California shouted.

But the figure didn't move.

"Get up, motherfucker!" California yelled. "I said, get up! *Now!*"

THIRTEEN

"**I** said, get up now, motherfucker!" California shouted.

When Somerset peered in from the doorway, all he could see were backs and heads, everybody focused on whoever was in that bed. He quickly scanned the rest of the room and couldn't figure out why there were so many air fresheners in there. They were all over the place, hundreds of them, plastic tubes and disks in a rainbow of pastel colors, some stuck to the wall, others clustered on a small table and two chairs, the rest on the floor. The place had an overpowering floral aroma, like potpourri hell. An old yellowed bed sheet was tacked to the wall that faced the foot of the bed. Then he noticed what was on the wall behind the door: SLOTH written in shit. Somerset automatically started breathing through his mouth even though the overwhelming sweetness of the air fresheners obliterated any possible stink.

California kicked the bed so hard one end lifted off the floor. "Get up!" Carefully he reached over, then quickly yanked the sheet off, a ripple going through the room as each man tensed, knowing that he might have to fire his weapon in the next millisecond. But the letdown was ghastly. What they saw definitely wasn't going to lash out at them.

"Oh, man . . ." California groaned, backing away.

Somerset moved in to get a better look. A nearly naked body lay on the bed, shriveled and covered with bed sores. It was a man, or more accurately the mummy of a man. The skin was the gray color of putty. The emaciated face was blindfolded, and he had been tied to the bed frame with thin wire that had been meticulously wrapped around him over and over again, like a fly that had been packaged by a spider. A stained loincloth covered the man's groin. Two tubes ran out from the loincloth and snaked their way under the bed.

"Jesus H. Christ . . ." the black cop mumbled.

Mills kept shaking his head, unable to take his eyes off the body. "Holy fucking shit . . ."

The stench from the uncovered body slowly rolled through the room, making Somerset take out his handkerchief. The air fresheners didn't stand a chance against this. He wedged his way in next to Mills and pulled out the photocopy of Victor Dworkin's mug shots.

"Is it him?" Mills asked.

Somerset compared the blindfolded face to the one in the pictures. It was the same pointed chin and hooked nose. "Yeah. It's him."

"Lieutenant, check this out." California pointed with the barrel of his gun at the man's right arm. The hand was gone—sawed off, actually, from the look of the wound, which had healed over long ago.

"Call an ambulance," Somerset said to California.

"You mean a hearse," California said. "This guy's long gone."

"Lieutenant? Take a look at this." The black cop had taken the yellowed sheet down from the wall. It was covered with Polaroid pictures of Victor lashed to the bed, a date neatly written on the bottom of each one. "There are fifty-two of them, Lieutenant. I counted."

Somerset went over to inspect them. It was a visual chronicle of Victor's gradual deterioration, his metamorphosis from an average-build with a small pot-belly to skin and bones. Somerset couldn't help but think of the photos he'd seen of World War II concentration camp survivors. "What's the date today?" he asked, his stomach turning.

"Ah . . . the twentieth," the black cop answered.

Somerset pointed to the date on the first picture. "The torture started exactly one year ago to the day. Christ almighty," he murmured. "What the hell kind of monster is this guy?"

Mills put away his gun and pulled out a pair of latex gloves. "Okay, California, get your people out of here. This is a homicide."

California glared at him, but only for a moment. "You heard the man," he said to his men. "Hit the hall, and don't touch anything on your way out."

Somerset squeezed between them before something started. California was as much of a hothead as Mills. Actually they deserved each other. Mills let his glare linger for a moment before he went over to check out the Polaroids. Somerset lifted the sheet and carefully covered Victor Dworkin up to the neck. California stood by.

"He looks like some kind of creepy wax dummy,"

California said. He was staring down at Victor's blind-folded face, mesmerized.

Somerset reached down to feel Victor's neck for a pulse on the off chance that his heart might still be pumping when Mills suddenly called him over. "Look at this. I can't fucking believe it." Mills was livid.

"What?" Somerset noticed California trying to peel back the sheet. "Leave it alone, sergeant," he snapped. "You're disturbing evidence."

California retracted his hand, still hypnotized by the gruesome sight of the body.

Mills was down on one knee. Under the sheet that had been on the wall he'd found an open shoe box. Printed on the side of the box in black marker was TO THE WORLD FROM ME. Somerset hunkered down to see what was inside.

Back at the bed, California was leaning over the gaunt face. "You got what you deserved, Victor."

Somerset barked. "Get away, sergeant!"

California stood up straight and moved back. "Sorry, Lieutenant."

Somerset ignored him and started going through the shoe box. He picked out one of several small Ziploc bags. It contained clumps of brown hair. The next bag had several tablespoons' worth of a yellow liquid.

"A urine sample," Mills said in disgust. "And a hair sample and a stool sample. Here—fingernails, too. He's laughing at us. The goddamn son of a bitch is laughing at us."

California had inched closer to Victor again, and Somerset was about to order him out of the room when suddenly a loud, guttural bark issued from the corpse, scaring the shit out of California. The sergeant stumbled back and tripped over a chair, spilling a dozen air fresheners all over the floor. Victor's mouth was open, the chin moving ever so slightly.

"He's alive!" California pointed at Victor's face. The sergeant's voice was up two octaves.

Somerset and Mills rushed to the blindfolded man. Victor's lips were trembling feebly. A faint gurgling sound issued from his throat.

"Oh, Jesus . . ." Mills said.

"He's still alive!" California repeated incredulously.

"Get an ambulance!" Mills shouted. "Right now!"

FOURTEEN

Ten minutes later California was barreling down the third-floor hallway, running interference for the two EMS workers racing behind him with a folded stretcher. "Out of the way!" he yelled. "Out of the way!"

But busybody neighbors had come out of their apartments, chattering and gawking, anxious to see what was going on, the whole place as crazy as a beehive. Mills and Somerset took up positions at the head of the staircase, determined to keep the distance between Victor's apartment and the stairs clear. The other uniforms were on the landings down below, doing the best they could controlling the crowd until backup arrived. Mills wanted to go back to the apartment, afraid that California and his damned curiosity would taint the crime scene, but Somerset had already pulled rank and ordered him to stay put right here.

"But, Lieutenant," Mills tried again, "don't you think I should go back in to make sure—"

"No."

"But the EMS guys are going to screw up evidence."

"They'll do that whether you're there or not. They've

got a life to save. And that life may be the only witness we'll ever get who can identify the killer." Somerset was getting annoyed with him.

"Excuse me, Officer." A young Hispanic man wearing jeans, no shirt, and sandals came up behind Somerset. Three small children followed him like ducklings. "What happened here?"

"We don't know yet," Somerset lied. "Please stand back. And take those children back inside."

The young man's face turned sour. He gave Somerset the finger behind his back, but then did what he was told and brought the kids back into their apartment.

"Did you see that?" Mills asked. "Did you see what that guy did?"

"I don't care what he did," Somerset said. "I don't worry about that kind of stuff."

Mills didn't like Somerset's attitude. What was he saying? That he had more important things to think about? "So what *do* you worry about?"

"Right now I'm worrying about this goddamn killer. I'm worried that we may have underestimated him." Somerset looked as if he had the weight of the world on his shoulders, and that pissed off Mills, too. He wasn't the only cop on this investigation. It wasn't up to him alone to catch this guy.

"I want him bad, too," Mills said. "You do understand that, don't you? I don't want to just catch him anymore. I want to *hurt* him."

Somerset looked him in the eye. "That's what this guy wants. Don't you understand that? He's playing games."

"No kidding! No fucking kidding!"

"Look, we have to divorce ourselves from our emotions here. No matter how hard it is, we have to stay focused on the details."

Mills pointed to his own chest. "I don't know about you, Lieutenant, but I *feed* off my emotions."

Suddenly Somerset grabbed him by the jacket. "Are you listening to me, Mills?!"

Mills pushed him away. "You know what your fucking problem is—hey!"

Mills covered his eyes as a camera flash suddenly blinded him. The sound of film automatically advancing came from the stairway below. Mills blinked, trying to regain his vision. A guy with a camera, a reporter, was standing in the middle of the stairs, pointing a camera up at them. Both Mills and Somerset shielded their eyes as he fired off three more shots in quick succession.

"What are your names, Officers?" the reporter called out. He had a thin, nasal voice. His suit was wrinkled, and he wore thick glasses. If he were a little balder, he'd be a ringer for Elmer Fudd.

You little fuck, Mills thought as he rushed down the stairs and grabbed the man by the lapels. "What the fuck're you doing here? How'd he get up here?" he yelled down to the uniform on the next landing.

The cop on the next landing was doing all he could to hold back the people clamoring to see what was going on upstairs. "I'm doing my fucking best, Detective!"

The reporter was squirming under Mills's grip. He managed to get ahold of the laminated press card hanging from a chain around his neck and waved it in Mills's face. "I'm UPI, Officer. I have—"

Mills saw red and shoved him hard. The reporter stumbled back and fell the last few steps to the landing below. "I don't give a shit what you have, pal. That card doesn't mean squat to me. This is a closed crime scene. You understand that?"

Somerset came down the steps and took Mills by the elbow, but Mills whipped his arm free. The reporter was shaking as he collected his camera and scrambled to his feet. "You can't do this!" he whined. "You can't!"

"Get the fuck out of here!" Mills shouted, and the reporter scurried down the stairs, his face as white as a ghost. Mills peered over the railing and followed his progress to make sure he disappeared.

"You'll be hearing from my lawyer!" the reporter yelled up as he rushed down the steps. "I've got your picture! I've got pictures of you!"

"Fuck you, you little—"

Somerset grabbed Mills and pulled him away from the railing, forcing him to sit down on the stairs. "Enough."

Mills raised his palms and let out a long breath. "All right, all right. But just tell me one thing. How do these cockroaches get here so quick?"

Somerset smirked as if he should know better. "They pay cops for tips, and they pay well."

Mills nodded. He let out another long breath to calm himself. "Sorry. I don't know, I just lost it . . . Sorry."

"Don't worry about it," Somerset said sarcastically. "I'm always impressed when I see a man feeding off his own emotions."

Mills clenched his jaw and glared at Somerset. *You son of a bitch—*

"Make way! Make way!" California yelled.

The EMS guys were bringing Victor Dworkin down. Mills rushed down to the next landing and squeezed into the corner so that they could get the gurney through. As they passed, he could see Victor's face, now without the blindfold. His eyes were sunken deep into his skull, but there was a moist glimmer behind the slits. He looked like a dried-out baby bird that had fallen from the nest, abandoned by its mother.

"Come on! Let's go! Let's go!" California barked.

As they brought the gurney around the turn in the landing, Mills had to press himself all the way into the corner to make room. Victor's face was just inches away, and Mills couldn't help but stare. Suddenly he noticed the eyes move. Victor was looking at him! He froze where he stood, his blood turning to ice.

Mills's heart was slamming in his chest. The fucking mummy had looked at him.

Victor Dworkin's color looked worse against the clean white hospital sheets than it did at his dingy apartment. His skin was dark and leathery, as if he had gone through a tannery. He lay motionless inside an oxygen tent, an IV drip connected to his neck, a blood transfusion going through his thigh. The room was dim, and a moist towel had been laid across his eyes. Mills listened to the bleep of his heart monitor. The bleeps were very far apart. Mills anticipated each one, fearing that the next one wouldn't come, that Victor would expire, and there would go their only eyewitness, the only person in the world who could point the finger at the killer.

Dr. Beardsley was huddled with Somerset on the other side of the bed, their images blurry and distorted through the clear plastic tent. The doctor had a bush of curly gray hair and an intense, bony face. Somerset nodded as the doctor spoke, jotting down everything the doctor was telling him in his notepad.

Mills stared at Victor's face through the plastic. He wanted Victor to wake up, but he dreaded the moment when he did. He knew it was going to be creepy, like something out of a horror movie. Mills just couldn't imagine how this guy could ever recover. If he did, he'd have to go through life looking like the Crypt-Keeper. He watched the monitors above the bed for a few minutes, but they were so slow, they were making him sleepy. Finally he got up and went over to the other side of the bed to hear what the doctor had to say.

". . . a year of immobility seems about right," he was telling Somerset, "judging from the extensive deterioration of the muscles and the spine. Blood tests show a whole smorgasbord of drugs in his system, even an antibiotic which must have been administered to keep the bed sores from becoming infected."

Mills looked into the tent and winced. A whole year lashed to that bed, he thought. A whole year at the mercy of that monster.

Somerset looked up from his pad. "Is there *any* chance he'll survive?"

"Let me put it this way, Detective. If you were to suddenly shine a flashlight in his face right now, he'd probably die of shock. Instantly."

Somerset clicked his ballpoint and put it away. Mills caught his eye, but there was nothing to say. Victor Dworkin wasn't going to be able to help them catch this bastard.

"Has Victor said anything, doctor?" Mills asked. "Has he tried to express himself in any way?"

Dr. Beardsley stuck out his bottom lip and shook his head. "Even if his brain weren't mush, which is essentially what it is, he couldn't speak if he wanted to."

"Why not?"

"He chewed off his tongue sometime during his ordeal. Most likely for the nourishment."

Mills looked at the floor and shook his head. If he hadn't felt so hollow, he would've thrown up.

FIFTEEN

That afternoon back at the precinct house, the Homicide bullpen smelled of stale cigarette smoke and burnt coffee. At the front of the room a battered podium faced a haphazard collection of secretarial and folding chairs. Two hulking gray desks had been pushed together against a side wall to serve as table space. Somerset stood by himself in front of the stand-up blackboard, staring at what he'd written on it during the briefing that had just broken up:

1. GLUTTONY
2. GREED
3. SLOTH
4. ENVY
5. WRATH
6. PRIDE
7. LUST

He shook the chalk in his hand as if he were warming up to shoot dice. He stepped forward and drew lines through GLUTTONY, GREED, and SLOTH. The captain had assigned three new men to the case, and at the briefing Somerset and Mills had brought them up to date on the status of the investigation. Somerset put down the chalk and glanced over at Mills, who was sitting by himself on a folding chair, reading through the initial canvass reports taken from people who lived in Victor Dworkin's building. Somerset wished the captain hadn't given them California. He and Mills were going to be like oil and water. Somerset could feel it. The chemistry between them was bad, and it was just a matter of time before those two had it out.

Somerset leaned on the podium. He also wished he could psyche himself up for this investigation. This killer had to be stopped, there was no question about that, but Somerset just didn't know if he was up to it. It wasn't that he couldn't do it so much as he didn't want to *make* himself do it. He was ready to retire, to get away from all this crap. But if he put himself through this again, he wasn't so sure that he'd ever be able to turn his back on the city. Who would catch the next monster? Mills? Not by himself. Not yet.

He picked up a sheaf of papers from the podium and wandered over to the windows. A rare cool breeze was blowing in. He leaned on the sill and tilted his head back, trying to enjoy it while it lasted. Simple pleasures didn't last long in the city.

"Did you read the landlord's statement?" he asked Mills.

Mills looked up from his reading. "No. What did he say?"

"He said an envelope of cash was in the office mailbox each month. He said, quote, 'I never heard a single complaint from the tenant in apartment 303, and nobody ever complained about him. He's the best tenant I've ever had.' "

Mills exhaled a humorless laugh. "A landlord's dream tenant, a paralyzed man with no tongue."

"Who always pays the rent on time," Somerset added.

"And in cash."

Somerset shook his head, once again amazed at how people can convince themselves that things are fine when they obviously aren't. The cash payments alone should've made the landlord suspicious. Who pays their rent in cash? Ten to one, the landlord wasn't declaring that money to the IRS. That's why he never questioned it.

Mills tossed the sheaf of reports he'd been reading onto the nearest desk. "I'm sick of sitting around waiting. I want to *do* something."

"Hey, this is what the job is all about," Somerset said. "Only Batman stops crimes before they happen."

"There must be something we can follow up on. I mean, do we have to let this lunatic make all the moves?"

Somerset didn't like hearing this. Mills wasn't getting it. "Don't dismiss him as a lunatic. That's too easy, and it's a big mistake."

"Aw, come off it, man. This guy's insane. Right now he's probably dancing around his room in a pair of his mommy's panties, rubbing himself with peanut butter."

Somerset shook his head. "No. Not this guy."

"What do you mean, 'not this guy'? You telling me you got a feel for him? A psychic connection? You feel what he's thinking? Hey, I saw that movie, too, and I know it's bullshit."

Somerset just stared at him. He'd assumed that Mills understood more about habitual killers than this. Mills had a lot to learn. There was no way he was going to be able to take over this investigation by himself.

"You know what I think?" Mills said. "I think this guy has been damn lucky so far, but sooner or later his luck is going to run out. And we just have to be there when it does."

Somerset could only shake his head. "He's not depending on luck. Luck has nothing to do with it. We walked into that apartment exactly one year after he first tied Victor Dworkin to his bed. One year to the day! He planned it that way. That's exactly what he wanted to happen."

"We don't know that for sure."

"Yes we do. Think. What were his first words to us? 'Long is the way, and hard, that out of hell leads up to the light.' "

"So?"

"He's true to his word. For him it has been long and hard. Just imagine the will it must have taken to keep Victor Dworkin alive and bound like that for a full year. To connect tubes to his penis, to empty his piss. To sever his hand and use it to plant fingerprints. To keep Victor tottering on the edge of survival without killing him. This man is methodical, exacting, and worst of all, he's patient. The way out of hell is long and hard, and this guy's got the stamina."

Mills made a face. "You know, you got Dante on the brain. You think all this literary, theological crap is the key to figuring this character out. It's not. Face it. Just because the bastard has a library card, that doesn't make him Einstein."

Library card, Somerset thought. Then something suddenly occurred to him. He stared out the window at the line of squad cars parked behind the precinct. Library card . . .

"What? What are you thinking?" Mills stood up and went over to him. "I know that look. I can see the wheels turning."

"You still itching to do something?" Somerset asked.

"Yeah, of course."

"How much money do you have on you?"

"I don't know, about fifty bucks."

Somerset checked his own wallet. He had eighty. "I propose we take a field trip."

"A what?"

"Come on."

In the reference room at the main branch of the public library, Somerset was staring at the print head of a dot-matrix printer grinding back and forth across the page as it printed out book titles one after the other. Mills stood behind him, arms crossed, looking bored. He felt very out of place here, and the two lady librarians behind the reference desk kept staring at him, like a pair of puff pigeons eyeing an alley cat. They seemed uneasy with his presence. *Well, frig them*, Mills thought. After several minutes, the printer finally stopped, and Somerset ripped off the printout, which was four pages long.

"Are you going to tell me what the fuck we're doing here, Lieutenant? We've got a psycho on the loose, and you're checking on your overdue library books."

"Not exactly," Somerset said as he folded the pages and tucked them into the inside pocket of his jacket. "Come on, let's go."

"Now where? A bookstore?"

"Patience, Mills. The killer has lots of it, and so should you. This will all become clear to you shortly." Somerset headed for the front doors.

Mills rushed to catch up. "Wait a minute, will you?"

"Ssshhhh!" A little old lady pushing a cart full of books scowled at Mills. "Be quiet, please!"

Mills gave her a dirty look. He almost gave her the finger, but stopped himself at the last moment. "Always hated fucking libraries," he muttered as he hurried to catch up with Somerset.

Somerset was already outside, moving down the library's stone steps. The sun was bright and warm outside, and Somerset seemed to be rejuvenated by this "field trip" to the library, but Mills didn't get it. He raced down the steps. "Hold up, Lieutenant."

Somerset stopped on the bottom step and looked back at him. "What's the matter?"

"What's the matter? First you drag me over here to look up books on fucking Dante and the seven deadly sins and the Catholic Church and murder and homicide and S&M and every other crazy piece of shit that floats into your head, and now you won't even tell me what you're up to. I told you you had Dante on the brain. If you think you're going to find answers to what this guy is up to in a library, you're whistling Dixie, pal."

Somerset just grinned, puckered his lips, and started to whistle the notes to "Way down south in the land o' cotton . . ." He went to the curb and crossed the street against the traffic.

"Motherfucker!" Mills cursed under his breath in frustration as he followed Somerset across.

On the other side of the street there was a line of

stores shoulder-by-shoulder—a discount merchandise store, a drug store, a wig store, a Radio Shack, and a pizza parlor. Outside the pizza parlor, a grizzled man in a tattered tan raincoat was passing out handbills. Pedestrians gave him a wide berth in order to avoid him. "Take one, you stupid fucks!" the man growled. "It's a coupon, for Chrissake. Take one! Save some fucking money! Here, take it."

Mills brushed past him, following Somerset into the pizza parlor.

"Just coffee," Somerset was saying to the man behind the white Formica counter as Mills came up behind him.

"A slice with pepperoni and a large root beer," Mills added. "I'll get it," he said to Somerset, reaching into his pocket.

"Thanks. I'll get a booth."

Somerset was poring over that printout from the library when Mills came over with their order. "Sit over here," he said. "Next to me."

"Why?" Mills said, still trying to figure out what Somerset was up to with this "field trip." "What, are we dating now?"

"I hope not," Somerset said, unperturbed. He was reading the printout.

Mills set down the brown plastic tray and did as he was told, taking a seat next to Somerset. He unwrapped a straw and stuck it into his drink, waiting for Somerset to get his face out of that printout and tell him something. But that didn't look like it was going to happen soon, so he picked up his slice of pizza and folded it over, about to take a bite.

"You really going to eat that?" Somerset asked disapprovingly.

"Well, what do you think I'm going to do with it?"

"This place had about fifty health code violations last time they were inspected."

"Now you tell me." Mills threw down the pizza as he visualized the size of the roaches that lived in his apartment. About as big as the pepperoni slices on his pizza and about the same color, only not so round. "Shit!" he grumbled.

Suddenly a greasy-looking character in a black suit and black shirt buttoned to the neck was hovering near their table. He wore rose-tinted aviator glasses, and his fingers were encrusted with gaudy rings. A cigarette burned in one hand. *What the fuck is this?* Mills thought. But when Somerset didn't react to the man's arrival, he assumed the lieutenant knew him.

"Let me have that fifty," Somerset said to Mills.

Reluctantly Mills reached into his pants pocket for his wallet and pulled out the bills. He stopped and checked out the man with the slicked-back hair again, still unsure about all this.

The man sucked on his teeth before he spoke. "We gotta problem here," he said to Somerset.

Somerset shook his head.

Mills sighed and passed the money to Somerset under the table. "I'm handing you this, and for some strange reason, I'm thinking that maybe I should know what the fuck we're doing here. Maybe it's just me, though. Maybe I'm the one who's strange."

Somerset combined Mills's money with some of his own, then folded it into the computer printout. He nodded to the greaseball in the black suit, indicating that he should sit down.

The man slipped into the booth opposite them.

"How's it goin', Somerset?" He flashed a slimy grin at Mills. "You didn't tell me this was gonna be a ménage à trois."

"It's not a problem," Somerset assured him.

"Only for you, my friend, do I do these things," the greaseball said. "Very big risk on my end, but I figure we'll be even after this. All fair and square."

"Probably," Somerset said as he passed the printout and the money under the table. The man unfolded the printout and glanced at the money before tucking it into his inside pocket. "In about an hour," the man said as he started to slide out of the booth. Before he left, he picked up Mills's slice of pizza and took a big bite. "No lunch," he said as he walked out with it.

After he left, Mills turned to Somerset, more confused than ever. "I'll bet that was money well spent, wasn't it?"

"Patience, Mills, patience. Come on, let's go."

The buzz of the electric clippers was getting on Mills's nerves. The old barber bent over his work, carefully shaving the back of his slightly younger customer's head. Mills was sitting in one of the waiting chairs, Somerset right next to him with a copy of *National Geographic* open on his crossed leg. It was an old-fashioned barber shop with bottles of hair tonics and cans of talc lined up on a long ledge under the mirror that ran the entire length of the shop. The barber, a squat black man with close-cropped steel-wool hair, looked old enough to have given Somerset his first haircut. Mills looked at Somerset. He was still waiting to find out what the hell they were doing on this stupid "field trip."

"What the fuck are we doing here, Somerset? I don't need a haircut."

Somerset looked up from under his brow, catching Mills's eye in the mirror. "Relax, Mills. Things happen when they happen. It's counterproductive to try to force results." He looked down at the magazine and flipped a page. "I want you to know, though, that by bringing you along on this little expedition, I'm trusting you more than I trust most people."

"Why don't you just get to the point and tell me what we're doing because I'm just about ready to punch something."

Somerset casually flipped few more pages, then looked at Mills sideways. "Ultimately this may not amount to anything, but if that's the case, then it's no skin off our teeth. That man back at the pizza parlor?"

"Yeah?"

"He's a friend of mine, at the Bureau."

"That greaseball is a feebie?"

Somerset nodded. "For a long time the FBI's been hooked into the library system, keeping track of the things."

"What kind of things? Overdue fines?"

Somerset ignored the sarcasm. "The feds monitor reading habits. Not every book is flagged, but certain ones are. Books about—let's say—building nuclear weapons. Or *Mein Kampf.* Whoever takes out a flagged book ends up having his library records fed to the Bureau from then on."

"You've got to be kidding."

"Nope. Flagged books cover every topic the Bureau deems questionable, from communism to violent crime."

"Is this legal? I mean, Jesus, just because you read about building a bomb doesn't necessarily mean you're going to do it."

Somerset shrugged. "Legal, illegal—the terms don't apply. The feds can't use the information directly, but it can be a useful guide in tracking down possible suspects. Remember, you can't get a library card without ID and a current phone bill."

Mills's mood was starting to brighten. Maybe Somerset had something here. If the killer was a bookworm—like him—this actually could lead to something. Somerset knew what he was doing all along. It would've been nice, though, if he had clued in his partner before now. "So they're running the list you put together at the library?" Mills asked.

Somerset nodded. "Say there's someone out there who's been taking out Dante, *Paradise Lost*, and the lives of the great martyrs as well as, say, *Helter Skelter* and *The Iceman*, then the Bureau's computer will give us a name."

"Yeah, but what if we end up picking up some college kid writing a term paper on crime in the Middle Ages versus crime in the twentieth century?"

"Well . . . at least we're out of the office," Somerset said. The man in the barber's chair stood up then, and the barber started to brush him off. "Why don't you get a haircut while we're waiting?"

Mills eyed the barber's latest work. The barber had taken off so much around the ears, the poor guy's head looked like a jug from the back. "I think I'll pass on the haircut," Mills said. "But tell me something. How did you know about all this? The feds aren't exactly known for their openness."

SEVEN

Somerset looked down at his magazine. "I don't know anything about this. And neither do you. That's why we're doing it this way."

As the barber pressed the keys of his ancient cash register and the drawer popped out with a ding, the greaseball from the FBI came through the door, beaming like a used-car salesman. He shut the door behind him and took the seat next to Somerset, handing him a thick sheaf of printout paper.

"Anything good?" Somerset asked.

"Yeah," the man said, "I think I found something for you."

SIXTEEN

A n orange-red sun was wedged between two office towers, sinking fast. Sitting behind the wheel of his car, Somerset flipped the sun visor down to block the direct rays, so he could keep reading. He was parked in a downtown lot across the street from the barber shop.

In the passenger seat Mills had his foot up on the dashboard, making little moaning-and-groaning noises as he scanned his half of the FBI computer printout. An empty can of root beer was on the floor where he'd left it. "What a waste of time," he complained. "There's nothing here."

"We're focusing," Somerset said without looking up from the page he was reading. He was getting a little annoyed with Mills's attitude. What the hell did he think police work was? It wasn't shooting from the hip like some kind of cowboy, that's for sure. It was being a nitpicker, looking for that one little thing that could nail a criminal's ass to the wall in court. Good detective work was in the details, not the broad strokes. But that didn't make any sense to Mills right now, and Somerset wondered if it ever would. Heads didn't come much harder than Mills's.

"Focusing," Mills mimicked. "Focusing on what? One tiny little area that may not get us anywhere."

"You have a better suggestion? Maybe we should pick up every priest and Dante scholar in town. Or how about going through all the mug books, looking for someone whose MO matches our killer? Think we'll find anybody there? Hey, I've only been doing this job here for twenty-five years. Maybe I forgot about someone who was into bizarre forms of retribution and ritualistic slayings based on arcane medieval literature. Maybe that one just slipped my mind."

"All right, all right. I get the point."

"Do you?"

Mills glared at him. Clearly he didn't like being told things. *Well, too bad*, Somerset thought. He had a lot to learn yet.

"And get your foot off my dashboard . . . please."

Mills put his foot down, but from the smirk on his face, Somerset could see that he wasn't doing anything about the attitude.

Somerset ignored him and went back to his printout. Now he was convinced that Mills wouldn't last a year on this job. *This time next year he'll be the head of security out in some mall in the suburbs. Guaranteed.*

Outside the car's windshield, office workers hurried to get home before the sun went down. Somerset always thought of them as Transylvanians seeking shelter before Dracula rose from his grave and started stalking the countryside for fresh blood. Of course, these poor people didn't know how close to the truth that was.

Somerset glanced over at Mills, feeling bad about the

way he'd prejudged him. Maybe he was being a little unfair. After all, Mills hadn't seen half the barbaric shit Somerset had seen in his life. Mills also had a healthy sense of moral outrage, something that had been burnt out of Somerset a long time ago. Maybe Mills's impatience for results wasn't so bad. It showed that his heart was in the right place. And for that reason alone, he might make a pretty good detective some day. If he could just get his head in line with his heart.

Somerset flipped another page on the connected computer sheets, scanning a new prospective candidate's column of books. This was a particularly long one. *The Divine Comedy, A History of Catholicism*, a book called *Murderers and Madmen, Modern Homicide Investigation, In Cold Blood* . . . He showed the page to Mills. "What do you think of this?"

Mills took a look at it, his brow furrowed as he scanned the list. "*Of Human Bondage?*"

"It's not what you think."

Mills pointed to one entry. "The Marquis de Sade, *Origins of Sadism?*"

"That is."

Mills ran his finger down the list. "*The Writings of Saint Thomas Aqu . . . Aquin—*"

"Saint Thomas Aquinas. He wrote about the seven deadly sins."

"How do you know?"

"I read a lot."

"I don't." Mills was scowling at him again.

"This is the longest list I've found that meets our criterion. How about you?"

"Definitely. Most of mine don't have more than four

or five entries. This one has"—Mills did a quick count—"over thirty."

Somerset turned the key in the ignition and started the engine. "So maybe we should go check this person out? What's the name?

Mills flipped back a page to get the name. "Jesus! You're not going to believe this."

"What?"

"His name is John Doe."

"John Doe, huh?" Somerset put the transmission into reverse and backed out of the space. "What's the address?"

It was dark by the time they found John Doe's apartment. It was on a narrow dead-end street that was only one block long, in a poor area that bordered on the student ghetto where a lot of the university kids lived. Somerset had parked on the avenue, figuring that residents of this tiny street would spot a strange car right away.

As they walked into the narrow street, Somerset noticed that John Doe's building wasn't quite as old as the rest of the structures on the block, but it was just as run-down. The vestibule was covered with cheap wood paneling that bowed out from the walls. A couple of nails could fix that, but it was the kind of thing that never got done because nobody gave a shit.

Somerset checked the grid of doorbell buttons. There was no name next to the buzzer for #6A, the apartment that was listed on the FBI printout, but it wasn't the only buzzer that didn't have a name.

"This is nuts," Mills said. "It's too easy. Life doesn't work this way." He reached past Somerset to ring the buzzer, but Somerset grabbed his wrist before he did.

"What? I thought you wanted to talk to this guy."

"Wait." Somerset went to the front door and tried it. It was locked, but there was a lot of play in it. He could see that it was a cheap lock. Feeding the edge of his printout between the edge of the door and the jamb, then pulling it up was all it took to unlock it. "We don't want to give him too much warning. Just in case." Somerset pushed his way in and held the door for Mills.

"You don't really think it could be him" Mills said. "I mean, come on."

"The world is a strange place, Mills. It's always the same, but it's always a surprise. Let's just go up and take a look at him, hear what he has to say for himself. You never know."

"Sure. 'Ah, excuse me, sir, but are you by any chance a serial killer?' "

"Sshhh!" Somerset couldn't believe how stupid Mills could be sometimes. These tiled hallways were like echo chambers. He may as well use a bullhorn to let John Doe know that they were on their way up. Somerset went over to the elevator and pressed the up button. The faint smell of dog shit was in the air. He looked all around and checked his shoes, then finally noticed that one of the two bicycles that were chained to the balustrade of the stairway had shit smeared on its back tire. Somerset frowned at it. Cleaning it off before bringing the bike in would've made too much sense, he thought sarcastically.

The elevator arrived with a distressingly loud bang. Somerset got on and held it open for Mills as he pressed the "six" button.

"What're you going to say to him when we get

there?" Mills asked as he got in.

"I was thinking maybe you should do the talking. Put that silver tongue of yours to work." Somerset wanted to see how Mills handled himself, see how good he was at coaxing information out people. Mills was probably pretty good at playing "bad cop," but Somerset couldn't imagine him being very subtle.

The elevator door opened with another clunk on the sixth floor. Mills was grinning. "Who told you about my silver tongue? You been talking to my wife?"

"How is Tracy? I should've called to thank her for dinner the other night."

"She's okay. She said she really liked you. She said you seemed too sensitive to be a cop."

Once upon a time he was too sensitive, Somerset thought. Not now. He was a human callus now. "She's a real gift, Mills. Be good to her."

"Every day, every way. Tracy is the best thing that'll ever happen to me, and I know it."

Somerset was impressed that Mills could come right out and say that. Most men had a hard time putting their feelings into words, especially when it came to their wives. Somerset had always had that problem himself.

Getting out on the sixth floor, they checked the apartment numbers and saw that 6A was at the front of the building. It was at the end of the hall, straight ahead. Mr. Doe probably had a commanding view of the street, Somerset figured, but even if he did see them come into the building, he didn't know who they were.

Mills went ahead and knocked hard on the door. "Silver tongue," he chuckled to himself, waiting for a response.

The moment stretched. Mills knocked again. Somerset heard a small creak, but it didn't come from the door to #6A. He looked back to see who the nosy neighbor was, but it wasn't an apartment door. It was the door to the emergency stairwell. A dark figure was standing in the shadows, absolutely still, just looking at them. Then Somerset saw the glint of a gun barrel poking out of the slit in the door.

"Mills!" he shouted.

The gun went off, three times in a row, muzzle flashes strobing the dim hallway as Somerset and Mills hit the floor simultaneously. The explosions rang in Somerset's ears. Daylight was streaming through the ragged new holes in the door to #6A. They were as big as pie plates. *Fuck!* Somerset thought. *Hollow-point bullets!*

"Son of a bitch!" Mills scrambled on his belly, going for his own gun.

The slit in the door abruptly closed as Mills lunged for it. Somerset's heart leapt. An image of Mills taking a hollow-point and him having to tell Tracy that her husband was dead flashed through his mind. But Mills was already through the door before Somerset could even think about stopping him.

Be careful, you stupid son of a bitch, he thought. He was worried for Tracy.

Mills ran down the steps, then jumped the last four to the landing, pausing to listen. John Doe's fleeing footsteps echoed up the stairwell. Mills glanced up to Somerset standing on the landing above, his gun out and pointed up. He looked a little stunned, and Mills wondered if he was all right, if he was up to this.

"What kind of gun was it?" Mills yelled up.

Somerset headed down the stairs. He wasn't listening.

"Damn it, Somerset. What kind of gun was it? How many bullets?" Mills started down the next flight, then stopped in the middle, waiting for an answer.

"I don't know," Somerset finally said. "Might've been a revolver. I'm not sure."

Mills kept moving down the stairs as he kept his eye on Somerset. Suddenly he tripped and fell, hitting the next landing hard and dropping his gun. "Fuck!"

"What's wrong?" Somerset shouted down to him.

"Nothing." He picked up his gun and kept going.

Somerset was following him down; Mills could hear him breathing hard behind him. The guy smoked, Mills thought, he was about to retire. He was in no shape for this. Mills stopped and looked up at Somerset across the stairwell. "What's he look like? Did you see him?"

"Brown hat," Somerset said, huffing and puffing. "Tan raincoat . . . like a . . . a trenchcoat."

Mills peered over the railing, down to the next floor. Doe was standing there, gun hand reaching for the sky. Mills jumped back just as the crack of the gunshot reverberated up the stairwell. It hit the wooden railing inches from Somerset's hand. The wood splintered, sending chips and shreds raining down the cavernous space.

Another shot whizzed by and ricocheted off something several floors above.

Mills crouched on the landing, waiting for another shot, but instead he heard a door opening and banging shut. Five, he thought, rushing down the stairs to the next floor. Five shots so far.

The number four was stenciled on the wall next to

the fire door. "Fourth floor!" Mills shouted up to Somerset. "Fourth floor!"

He whipped the door open and went in, leading with his gun, sweeping right and left. At the far end of the hallway, John Doe was just turning the corner. Mills took off, sprinting after him. He took the turn and suddenly panicked, hoping to God Doe wasn't just standing there, waiting for him.

But Doe wasn't lying in wait. He was halfway down the next hallway, running full tilt.

Mills planted his feet, gripped his gun in both hands, closed one eye, and drew a bead on Doe's back, ready to squeeze one off and drop the guy. But suddenly a man in his T-shirt and underwear came out of his apartment, getting in the line of fire. "Get down!" Mills roared. "Get down! Move!"

But the man froze, too scared and confused to get out of his own way. Mills ran past him, shoving him aside.

Up ahead, a woman in jeans and a white sweatshirt poked her head out of her doorway just as John Doe was approaching. He stopped and grabbed her by the hair, pulling her out and throwing her against the wall.

"Hey!" she screamed.

Doe ran into her apartment.

"Get away!" Mills shouted. "Police! Don't go in there!"

He tore off in her direction and pushed her clear of the doorway before he kicked the door open all the way and entered, sweeping the room with his gun. It was a railroad flat, one room right after another. Straight ahead he could see John Doe climbing out the window onto the fire escape, and for a split second Mills froze, remembering the night they came for Russell Gundersen, the night Rick Parsons took a bullet on the fire escape and fell three stories, the night Rick became a cripple. Mills's hands began shaking. This was right where he had been standing that night, at the front door, facing the fire-escape window.

"Police! Stand clear!" It was Somerset out in the hallway. He was coming this way.

Mills couldn't let what happened to Rick happen to Somerset. He tore through the apartment to that window, intent on stopping Doe.

The door to the last room in the apartment started to close with the breeze from the open window. Mills bashed through it, knocking it off its hinges. White lace curtains swayed. He rushed to the side of the window, pressing his shoulder to the wall. Cautiously he crouched down and peered over the sill, craning his neck so he could see down into the alley. A gunshot shattered the open window, sending broken glass down onto his head and into his hair as he pulled back.

He sat with his back to the wall, panting, thinking, *Six! That's six shots. He's empty.*

Mills went back to the window, gun first, ready to blast the shit out of this son of a bitch when three more shots rang out, splintering both window sashes.

Mills dropped back inside. "Fuck!" he spat. "Seven, eight, nine. Some fucking revolver, Somerset."

Again, he went to the window, more cautious this time, but now he could hear running footsteps. He leaned outside and saw Doe escaping out the alleyway.

"Shit!" Mills shouted as he headed down the narrow fire-escape steps. "He's getting away!" He looked over the side. A car was parked under the fire escape. *What the fuck*, he thought, and vaulted over the railing, falling three and a half stories onto the roof of the car. The windshield shattered, and the roof collapsed, but it broke his fall. He hopped down and ran for the top of the alley, praying to God that he hadn't lost the bastard.

But when he reached the street, he wanted to scream. There were people everywhere—teens hanging out, little kids running all over the place, old ladies trudging down the sidewalk, mommies pushing strollers, guys just taking up space. He looked down the block, but it was hopeless. There was no way he could pick out a tan trenchcoat and a brown hat in this mob. He leapt up on a fire hydrant, grabbing hold of a NO PARKING sign for balance, and squinted into the distance.

Suddenly, impossibly, Mills spotted him. Brown hat and tan trench coat. He was at the corner at the end of the block, waiting for a break in the traffic so he could cross against the light.

Mills jumped down and ran into the street, waving off the oncoming traffic. Brakes screeched as drivers swerved around him.

"What the fuck is wrong with you?" one driver yelled.

Mills ignored him, cutting across the lane so he could run down the middle of the road. Cars and trucks whizzed past him in both directions. Too many people on the sidewalk, he figured. This was the fastest way.

A truck driver slowed down to shout at him. "Get out of the fucking road, you stupid ass. You're gonna get yourself killed."

Mills didn't bother with him. He had to keep his focus on John Doe or else he'd lose him.

But Doe heard the squealing tires and honking horns,

and he saw Mills coming. He quickly dashed across the street, forcing the oncoming cars to stop him, then ducked into another alley.

Mills abruptly crossed over to cut him off, trusting that the traffic would stop for him. A woman in a white Firebird came within inches of cutting him off at the knees. "What is wrong with you, man? Jesus!"

Mills didn't slow down. He went straight for the alley. It was narrow and dark, the buildings very close together, just a sliver of light beaming through at the far end. His eyes had to adjust from the bright sunshine. The alley was littered with trash cans and refrigerator boxes, homes for the homeless.

"Doe!" he yelled as he ran. "Police!"

No response. No sound in the alley at all, just his own running footsteps.

"Doe! You're under—"

It came out of the blue and hit him square in the face. Mills dropped his gun—he heard it clatter into a puddle—then he fell, first to his knees, then flat on his face, as the pain sapped all his strength. *A board, a fucking two-by-four,* he thought. He didn't see it coming, but through the overwhelming pain that was crushing his face, that was all he could imagine. Doe must've been hiding behind one of those big cardboard boxes, waiting for him. The pain expanded through his skull, doubling as it traveled. He squeezed his eyes shut and clutched his face. His nose was broken, he was sure of it. He coughed and spat. Blood was starting to fill his throat. He turned over on his side and kept spitting out blood.

Struggling to open his eyes, he heard the sound of wood hitting the pavement, like a baseball bat being thrown aside. A pair of legs were nearby. He saw a hand reach down and pick his weapon out of the puddle. Mills tried to reach out and grab it back, but he couldn't move. The pain was paralyzing.

Mills started coughing again, out of control, the blood choking him.

When he finally stopped coughing, he suddenly realized that there was metal touching his face, the barrel of his own gun stroking his cheek. He froze, helpless to do anything.

The gun gently traced circles around his cheeks and eyes, slid down the slope of his nose, outlined his mouth. Then it pried its way between his lips and roughly forced his jaws open. Mills tried to look into Doe's face, but blood was streaming into his eyes. An all-too-familiar sound nearly stopped Mills's racing heart: the click of his own gun's hammer as it was being cocked.

Mills coughed with the barrel in his mouth—he couldn't help it. A flash of white light hit him in the face, and for an instant he thought he'd taken a bullet through the brain. But he could still feel the barrel in his mouth, the blood in his eyes. He was still coughing. He wasn't dead.

After a long moment, the gun slowly withdrew from his lips. Mills was shaking, unable to move, unable to see. Suddenly something hit his chest, then another thing, and another and another. Bullets. They rolled off him and scattered on the ground. The bastard was emptying his weapon, laughing at him. His empty gun hit the asphalt as Doe's departing footsteps grew fainter and fainter.

Mills propped himself up on his elbow, gasping for breath, scared and furious. He swiped the blood from

his eyes with his sleeve and felt around for the gun and
the bullets like a blind man.

"Mills!" It was Somerset at the top of the alley. Mills
could hear him running toward him. "You all right?"
Somerset yelled. He rushed over and knelt down next
to him. "I'll call for an ambulance."

"No!" Mills said, rolling over and getting to his
knees. "I'm fine." He clenched his face against the pain
and climbed to his feet.

"What happened?"

Mills bent over and picked up the rest of the bullets.
He fed them back into the empty clip, counting them
in his head as they went in, imagining them going into
John Doe's gut.

"Mills? Talk to me. What happened?"

But Mills was too angry to talk. He had to get that
son of a bitch. There was no time for explanations. He
had to get him now. He started jogging toward the end
of the alley where a lone sliver of light beamed through,
like a sign from heaven. He ran as fast as he could,
despite the pain, heading in the direction that Doe had
taken. He was going to get that bastard. He swore to
Christ he would, and he'd make him suffer, the son of
a bitch. He would make him suffer.

"Mills! Where the hell're you going?"

But Mills didn't stop, and he didn't look back. He
was on a fucking mission.

"Mills!"

SEVENTEEN

As Mills burst out of the elevator on the sixth floor of John Doe's building, Somerset tried to grab his sleeve, but he whipped his arm back and shrugged out of it.

"Slow down, Mills. You hear me? Mills!"

But Mills charged ahead without a word, Somerset doing his best to keep up with him. All the way over here, Somerset had been trying to get Mills to tell him what had happened in the alley, but it was no use. The kid was a mad bull, and he was going to do something stupid, Somerset could feel it.

Mills's face was encrusted with blood, his nose swollen, bruises gaining color under his eyes. He was heading for the bullet-riddled door to apartment #6A, John Doe's apartment.

"Mills! Do not touch that door. Do you hear me, Mills?" Somerset ran up and grabbed his arm, not letting him go this time. "Wait, goddamn it! Just wait!"

Mills wheeled around and turned on him. "Why?" he snarled. "That was him, goddamn it! That was our guy!"

Somerset pointed at the splintered door. "You can't go in there."

"The hell I can't. We get in there, we can stop him."

"We need a warrant. You know that."

"Fuck that!" Mills pointed to his mangled face. "How the hell much probable cause do we need?" He tried to bull his way to the door.

But Somerset wasn't letting go. He grabbed Mills by the jacket and threw him against the wall. "Think!"

Mills struggled to break free. "What the fuck is wrong with you, man? Get off me!"

But Somerset had him pinned. "Think about how we got here, Mills." He pulled the crumpled sheaf of computer paper from the FBI out of his pocket and shoved it into Mills's chest. "We can't tell anyone about this. The Bureau will never acknowledge the library search, so we have no reason for being here. *We have no probable cause.*"

Mills was breathing hard, seething. "By the time we clear a fucking warrant, someone else is going to be dead. You know that, don't you?"

"Think, Mills, think. If we go in there without a warrant, we'll never be able to use anything we find in there. It'll be inadmissible in court. He'll walk."

Mills grabbed Somerset by the lapels, still struggling to break free. "Someone else will die. Can you live with that? I can't."

Somerset rammed him against the wall to make him stop, but deep down he knew that Mills was right. But, on the other hand, if the killer walked because they screwed up, entering his apartment without a warrant, then he'd kill again and again and again. "Look," he finally said, "we have to come up with some excuse for knocking on *this* door. You understand what I'm saying?"

Mills relaxed. "Okay, okay, I understand."

Somerset let go of him. But no sooner than he did, Mills wheeled around and kicked the door in.

Somerset wanted to kill him. "You stupid son of a bitch!"

Mills shrugged, wiping blood from his nose with the back of his hand. "No point arguing anymore. Unless you can fix it." The door jamb was cracked and splintered, the door creaking on its hinges.

The stairwell doorway where John Doe had been hiding suddenly banged open. Both men instantly drew their weapons.

"What the hell's going on here, huh? Why don't you two fairies go someplace else? Man can't get no peace nowhere nowadays." An emaciated old homeless man was tottering in the doorway, eyes unfocused, stinking of body odor and malt liquor. "C'mon, gimme a break over here. All's I want is a little peace and quiet. *A little peace and quiet!*"

Mills shifted his gaze to Somerset. "How much money do you have left?"

Half an hour later, a uniformed cop was taking the old homeless man's statement out in the hallway, writing down all the particulars. Mills stood behind the uniform, nodding demonstratively, encouraging the old guy with his eyes.

"So, so, so I . . . I noticed this guy going out," the old man sputtered, "going out a lot when those murders were happening. You know, the ones everybody's been talking about? So, so I . . . I . . ."

The old guy was still half in the bag, but he knew Mills had a twenty dollar bill with his name on it in his pocket, so he wanted to do good.

"So you called Detective Somerset," Mills prompted. "Isn't that what you told me? Someone on the street gave you his number."

"Yeah, right, I called the detective. Somerville."

"Who gave you Lieutenant Somerset's number, sir?" the cop asked.

The old man shrugged, eyes popping out of his long, drawn face. "Some guy. I dunno his name. Sleeps out in the same alley as me sometimes."

"You have any idea what his name is? Even a nickname."

The old man shook his head. "I call him Bud . . . I call everybody Bud."

The uniform glanced at Mills. "Yeah, this Bud's on me," he muttered sarcastically.

Mills just shrugged. "Hey, what can you do?" Inside, he was impatient to get this over with.

The uniform turned back to the old man. "So why did you call a detective, sir?"

"Because of this guy. He seemed so, so . . . creepy. And, and . . ."

Mills nodded, coaxing him to continue.

"And one of the murders was near here. Just a couple of blocks over. You know, the one who was still alive. Papers said he died in the hospital. You know, the one with the hand cut off. I just got to thinking, this guy who lives here in this building, him being so creepy and all, he could be the one who . . . you know . . ."

"And what did you *see*?" Mills said before the man got off the subject.

"I, ah . . . I saw . . . I saw him with one of those big spic knives, a machete. He had it under his coat, but he dropped it one day out in the alley, and I saw it."

"I told you the rest," Mills cut in before the man got too creative. The old guy's eyes were getting wild, and he'd already muttered something about extraterrestrials before the uniform arrived, so Mills wasn't going to take any chances. "The date that he saw the suspect drop the machete is consistent with the date that the ME estimates Victor Dworkin lost his hand. You need anything else?" he asked the uniform.

"No. This is good." He handed the clipboard and a pen to the old guy. "Just sign here . . . Bud."

Mills took the clipboard and made sure the old man scribbled something down in the right place. It took him a while, but he managed a fairly credible signature, all things considered. The uniform took his clipboard back. "Where's the lieutenant?" he asked Mills.

"Inside." Mills nodded toward the broken door to the apartment.

After the cop went in, Mills pulled out the twenty and showed it to the old guy. "Get something to eat with this," Mills whispered in his face. "Don't drink it. You understand me?"

"Yes, yes, yes." The man snatched the twenty and shoved it into his coat pocket. "Take it easy, Bud," he said as he scuttled through the stairwell doorway.

Mills just shook his head, knowing damn well that the old guy was going to drink himself silly with that money. Good thing he only gave him twenty. Somerset had wanted to give him more.

Mills pulled out a pair of latex gloves and headed into John Doe's apartment. The living room was unnaturally dark because the walls were painted black. So were the windows. Somerset and the uniform were huddled by a standing lamp, going over the old guy's statement. Mills and Somerset had already agreed on a story, that the old guy had heard screams coming from the apartment. They went to investigate. When there was no answer, they broke in on the chance that someone was in danger inside. Somerset wasn't happy with any of this, but he'd assured Mills that he could make it fly.

Except for the stand-up lamp and a lone ladder-back chair, the living room was totally empty. Mills moved on to the hallway, squinting into the darkness. He stopped at the first door he found and paused, wondering if he should take out his gun. Doe couldn't be here—unless he'd turned into a bat and flew in through a window—but Mills still had an uneasy feeling in the pit of his stomach. He kept his gun in its holster, but put his hand on the butt as he turned the knob. This room was pitch-black, too. Cautiously he felt for the wall switch, thinking about Victor Dworkin's severed hand, ready to pull his back at the first sign of trouble.

He found the switch and flipped it on. A harsh 100-watt bulb overhead illuminated another sparsely furnished room, walls and windows painted black. The single bed against the wall had no mattress, only a metal frame with safety-net-type springs. A worn sheet was neatly turned down at the head of it, but there were no pillows. The sheet had large sweat stains that were dotted with rust marks.

Dead center in the middle of the room there was a desk with a small banker's lamp on top. Mills pulled the chain to turn it on. There was nothing else on the desk at all.

He pulled back the straight-back chair and opened the middle drawer. A black leather-bound copy of the Holy Bible was all by itself in there. He opened the top right-hand drawer. It was full of empty aspirin bottles arranged standing up like a neat platoon. Mills did a quick count. There were about forty of them.

The next drawer contained three boxes of bullets, different kinds but all 9mm: semi-wadcutter hollow points, mercury-filled, and Teflon-coated. Teflon bullets were called "cop killers" on the street because they were designed to pierce body armor. Mills touched his bruised face, regretting that he didn't get the bastard when he'd had the chance.

Mills noticed a narrow endtable in the far corner of the room. It held a small stage, like a kid's school project, made out of a cardboard box and colored construction paper. A semicircle of overlapping Communion wafers had been artfully pasted to the back wall of the little stage. The wafers haloed the centerpiece of the work: a mayonnaise jar containing a human hand in a cloudy liquid.

Victor, Mills thought, unconsciously rubbing his own wrist. *Oh, man . . .*

"Lieutenant," he called out, going to the doorway. "I want you to see something."

"One minute," Somerset called back. He was still huddled with the uniform.

Standing in the doorway, Mills suddenly noticed something peculiar coming from down the black-walled hallway. A red glow was seeping out from under the bottom of a closed doorway at the end of the hall. Slowly he went toward it, feeling a little nauseous as he imagined what else he could find—other body parts, heads, feet, fingers, eyes, ears, genitals. He turned the knob and opened the door very slowly. It was the bathroom, illuminated by a red light over the medicine-cabinet mirror. Strips of film hung from the shower-curtain rod. Doe had converted his bathroom into a darkroom.

Finished prints covered every inch of wall space. Mills was overwhelmed by the sight. There were pictures of Peter Eubanks, the fat man, still alive; Eli Gould cutting into his own flesh; Victor Dworkin wasting away, his face pleading with the camera for mercy. There were also pictures of a glitzy blonde sitting on a bed. She wasn't dead or hurt, but she looked very uncomfortable. There were pictures of body parts, too, close-ups of mouths and fingers, but still attached. As he moved from picture to picture, Mills was struck by how much work and preparation Doe had put into his killings. Then he noticed something hanging from the toothbrush holder over the sink. A laminated UPI press ID on a chain.

"You fucking little asshole . . ."

He scanned the walls quickly, hoping he wouldn't find what he suspected. But he did, on the wall right over the toilet. Photos taken out in the hallway outside Victor Dworkin's apartment, photos peering into the crime scene from outside, photos of Somerset and Mills getting out of a car, photos of Somerset and Mills entering Victor's building, photos of them on the stairway when they were guarding the crime scene.

Mills pounded the sink with his fist. "Shit!" That silly-looking reporter, the guy who looked like Elmer Fudd. That was him. *I had him*, Mills thought, his gut burning.

I fucking had him, and I let him go. Son of a fucking bitch! Goddamn it!

Suddenly a phone rang. It was coming from somewhere down the hallway. Mills rushed out of the bathroom. Somerset and the uniform were coming the other way down the hallway. "I can't tell where it's coming from," Somerset said.

"You take the kitchen," Mills said. "And you," he said to the uniform, "don't touch anything unless you're wearing these." He pulled an extra pair of latex gloves out of his pocket and tossed them to the uniform.

The phone was on its third ring. Mills dashed into the bedroom. It was a weird muffled sound, but it seemed to be coming from in here. He opened the closet. It was full of clothes, but the ringing wasn't coming from in there. He got down on his hands and knees to look under the bed. He found a metal dome with a wooden knob on top. It took him a second to realize that this was the lid for a wok. A thin wire was trailing out from under it. Mills slid it out from under the bed and lifted the lid to reveal a black rotary phone underneath. It was sitting on a folded towel. Cotton batting had been glued to the inside of the lid to muffle it further. It rang once more. Mills reached into his jacket for his micro-cassette recorder, checking visually to make sure he had room on the tape. There was enough. He pressed the red "play" button, watched the wheels turn for a second, then picked up the receiver, holding the tape recorder to earpiece.

"Hello?" he said into the phone.

Silence. Someone was there, but he wasn't saying anything.

"Hello."

"I admire you," a nasal male voice finally said. "I don't know how you found me, but imagine my surprise. I respect you law-enforcement agents more and more every day. I really do."

"Okay, John," Mills said, "tell me—"

"No, no, no! You listen to *me*. I'll be readjusting my schedule in light of today's little setback. I just had to call and express my admiration. I'm sorry that I had to hurt one of you, but I'm afraid I didn't have a choice. You will accept my apology, won't you?"

Mills was seething, but he didn't answer.

"I feel like saying more," Doe continued, "but I don't want to ruin the surprise."

"What're you talking about, John?"

"Until the next time."

"John! Don't hang up! I—"

The dial tone filled the silence.

"Shit!" He hung up the phone and set it down on the floor.

Somerset was waiting in the doorway, a grave look on his face. He nodded toward the other rooms down the hall. "Wait'll you see what I found."

EIGHTEEN

Later that night John Doe's apartment was crammed with forensics people, and there was plenty of weirdness to keep them all going. Two techies dusted for prints while another examined Doe's little shrine to Victor's hand. A fourth was doing a careful inventory of Doe's desk. A sketch artist was in the kitchen with Mills, working up a likeness of Doe—or "Elmer Fudd," as Mills kept calling him—based on his recollections from their encounter on the stairway at Victor Dworkin's building. But while all this was going on, Somerset had kept himself cloistered in the apartment's second bedroom, John Doe's "library."

Bookshelves covered three walls in the room. Doe's selections said a lot about him, but nothing that didn't surprise Somerset: *A History of Theology, Handbook of Firearms, History of the World, Combat Ammunition, The Anarchist Cookbook, Summa Theologica, United States Criminal Law Review* . . . But the notebooks were another story.

One entire wall of bookshelf space was devoted to John Doe's personal notebooks, literally thousands of them. Each one contained roughly 250 pages, and both sides of each page were completely covered with writing and pastings, both original photographs cut from contact sheets and pictures that had been cut out of newspapers and magazines. Mills had dismissed the notebooks as "crazy shit" when Somerset had shown them to him, but Somerset disagreed. They were both horrifying and fascinating. Somerset kept picking through them, searching for clues and nuggets, gradually piecing together a portrait of John Doe's psyche. Somerset hadn't left the room since he'd brought Mills in to see it hours ago. Doe's writings—his musings, his philosophies, his thumbnail sketches—it all scared the shit out of Somerset. But not because it was bizarre and grotesque. Because on a certain level, Somerset agreed with Doe.

Doe was sick of all the dehumanizing crap people were forced to put up with these days, just like Somerset. The only difference was, Somerset had chosen to escape while Doe opted for the big statement. In his own demented way, he was taking the braver course, Somerset felt. He wasn't turning his back on the problems he saw; he was trying to change things with a great big wake-up call that no one could ignore.

As Somerset replaced one notebook and pulled out another, Mills came into the room. He was carrying a shoe box. "I've got good news and bad news," he said.

Somerset eyed the shoe box suspiciously, remembering the shoe box full of samples from Victor Dworkin's apartment. He wondered what—or who—Doe could have stuck in there. "Start with the good. I don't need any more negativity," Somerset said.

Mills took the lid off the shoe box and showed it to

him. To Somerset's surprise, it was full of cash, loose stacks of worn dollar bills, mostly hundreds and fifties. "Doe's slush fund," Mills said. "If this is his only source, he may be hurting for cash now."

"Maybe." Somerset was skeptical. Doe thought things through. It was evident in the meticulous way he planned his murders. He'd most likely have a reserve account somewhere. "So what's the bad news?"

"We haven't found any fingerprints yet. Not a single one. Either he wears gloves around the house, or he burned them off with acid."

"Keep looking," Somerset said. "Any luck getting us a few more men?"

"I called the captain. He said he wanted to come down and see for himself before he started reassigning people."

"This is all he needs to see." Somerset nodded at the shelves of notebooks. "There must be two thousand of these things. We need to go through all of them. I think he's trying to tell us something."

"Does he write about the murders?"

"Not directly. Not that I've found so far."

"So what does he say?"

Somerset opened to a page at random and started to read. " 'What sick, ridiculous puppets we are, and what a gross, little stage we dance on. What fun we have, dancing and fucking, not a care in the world. Not knowing that we are nothing. We are not what was intended.' " Somerset flipped a few pages. " 'On the subway today, a man came to me to start a conversation. He made small talk, this lonely man, talking about the weather and other things. I tried to be pleasant and accommodating, but my head began to hurt from his banality. I almost didn't notice that it had happened, but I suddenly threw up all over him. He was not pleased, and I couldn't help laughing.' "

"I'd rather read Dante," Mills said.

Somerset closed the book. "There are no dates that I can find. They're placed on the shelves in no discernible order. It's just his mind poured out on paper. If we had fifty men reading these on twenty-four-hour shifts, it would still take two months to get through them all."

Mills scanned the shelves and shook his head. "His life work."

Somerset had an urge to read them all himself. Doe's thoughts were revolting, but they were also intriguing. Doe was bothered by some of the same things that bothered Somerset. Maybe reading Doe's thoughts would help Somerset sort out his own, figure out where he belonged in this life. He didn't dare share this with Mills, though. Mills wouldn't understand. Somerset wasn't sure *he* understood.

"Did you find anything else?" Somerset asked.

"Yeah." Mills pulled a couple of plastic evidence bags out from under the shoe box. The top one had a picture of a sleazy-looking blonde standing on a street corner at night. Beneath the makeup and the hooker get-up, she was actually quite attractive. "There are pictures of her hanging up in the bathroom along with the pictures of Doe's victims."

Somerset stared at her face and sighed. Having a place in Doe's gallery wasn't a good sign. "Anybody have any idea who she is? She looks like a pro."

Mills shook his head and shrugged. "Whoever she is, she caught John Doe's eye."

"Let's put it out over the wire, and check with Vice.

Maybe they know who she is. Maybe we'll get lucky and find her while she's still breathing. What else do you have?"

"This." Mills shuffled the evidence bags and put the blonde on the bottom. "This was in Doe's desk with a bunch of bills and papers."

Somerset took the evidence bag. Inside there was a pink receipt from Wild Bill's Leather Shop. The total was for $502.64. "Custom job—paid in full," was handwritten across the front.

Somerset checked his watch. It was past eleven. Wild Bill was probably closed for the night. He handed the receipt back to Mills. "We'll check this out in the morning. In the meantime, go home and get some sleep."

"You going home?"

Somerset nodded as he put the notebook back where he'd found it. "Just make sure you sleep with the phone between your legs, Mills. John Doe's been rousted. Unfortunately now he's on the move."

An hour later Somerset was lying in bed, listening to the tick of his metronome, staring at the wallpaper rose in his hand. It was going to be a bad night, he could tell. He knew he wasn't going to get to sleep anytime soon, and he was too wired to concentrate on a book. Unless it was one of John Doe's notebooks. He couldn't stop thinking about some of the things he'd read. Doe made a lot of sense in his warped way, but Somerset didn't want him to make sense. He wanted Doe to be a raving loony tune. But he wasn't. The man was intelligent, and he had some very legitimate complaints.

The thump of a boombox out on the street competed with the steady rhythm of the metronome. It was driving him to distraction. Somerset was tempted to go out and smash the goddamn thing. Didn't those stupid kids have any consideration for anyone? But Somerset knew they didn't, so what was the use even thinking about doing anything? How do you resolve something like this? Destroy their boombox? Or, no, maybe do what John Doe would do—destroy *them*. On the other hand, you could do what Somerset was planning to do—just run away and let these animals thrive and multiply, let the city destroy itself while he grew flowers in the country. He fingered the wallpaper rose, rubbing it hard, wondering if he was really doing the right thing leaving this all behind.

The thumping rap rhythm expanded in his head, blocking out all rational thought. But if you couldn't think, you weren't human, and if your humanity was taken away, what was left? A long slide back down the evolutionary chain, that's what. Damn it all, he thought, rubbing his temples, you just can't let things go. Some things have to be confronted. If something is wrong, it's wrong. Confront it. Correct it.

Somerset tossed the wallpaper rose onto the night-stand and threw back the covers. He went to the closet for a pair of pants, intent on showing those fucking kids how to behave. He zipped up his pants and stepped into a pair of loafers, then without thinking, took his gun in its holster from the top of the bureau and started to shrug into it over his T-shirt. Suddenly he froze when he caught a look at himself in the mirror. He started breathing hard, a cold sweat beading his forehead.

What the hell was wrong with him? he thought. What was he going to do, shoot them? Christ Almighty, was he turning into John Doe?

The phone rang, and he jumped. He quickly took off his holster and grabbed the receiver in the middle of the second ring.

"Hello?"

The metronome ticked.

"Hello, William? It's Tracy."

He glanced at the alarm clock. It was after midnight. "Tracy, is everything all right?"

"Yes, yes. Everything's fine."

"Where's David?"

"He's in the shower. I'm sorry to call you so late."

"No, it's all right. I was up." Somerset sat down on the edge of the bed.

"I . . . I need to talk to someone, William. Can you meet me somewhere? Maybe tomorrow morning?"

Somerset switched the phone to his other ear. "I don't understand, Tracy. You sound upset."

"I feel really stupid, but you're the only person I really know here. There's no one else."

"I'll help you if I can, Tracy." He wasn't sure what she was getting at.

"So can you get away tomorrow? Just for a little while, so we can talk?"

"I don't know, Tracy. This case is keeping us pretty busy." He couldn't imagine why she was calling him, of all people. What could he do for her?

"Well, if you can get away, please call me. Please. David's getting out of the shower. I have to go now. Good night." She hung up.

Somerset hung up the phone and stared at the metronome. It was still ticking. Outside the boombox was still thumping.

Tracy's call had bothered Somerset all night, so the next morning he called her and told her to meet him early at the Parthenon Coffee Shop around the corner from the precinct house. When Somerset got there, the place was bustling with office workers clamoring for faster service, so they could make it to work on time. Tracy was in a booth by the plate-glass window, staring sadly into the rising steam from a cup of coffee. He slid into the seat across from her.

"Good morning," he said as he slid into the booth.

She looked up and blinked, suddenly realizing where she was. "Oh . . . William. Hi." She forced as best a smile as she could.

Somerset waved to Dolores, the sourpuss waitress who always waited on him. She knew to bring him his usual. Coffee and a buttered roll. "So. What's on your mind, Tracy?"

Tracy sighed. "I . . . I don't know how to begin."

"Well . . . start with what's on your mind. You'll get around to what's bothering you eventually." He wanted to be upbeat and understanding for her, but he was faking it. John Doe was the main thing on his mind, and he wanted to get back to the precinct house as soon as possible. He had a lot to do.

"You know this city," she finally started. "You've been here for a long time. I haven't."

Somerset nodded, trying to be sympathetic. "It can be a hard place."

"I haven't been sleeping very well since we moved here. I don't feel safe. Even at home."

Somerset could only nod. He didn't know what to tell her. Maybe her pigheaded husband should've talked it over with her before they'd made the big move to the city.

An awkward silence fell over them. He glanced at the watch on her wrist. It was getting late. He should be getting back to work.

The waitress brought his breakfast. He made himself busy, putting milk and sugar into the coffee, scraping the excess butter off the roll. He was waiting for her to get to the point, but she was still stuck, searching for the right words. "I feel a little strange being here with you," he said. "Without David knowing."

"I'm sorry. It's just that I had to talk to—"

There was a loud banging on the window. Somerset looked up to see two punks in homeboy parkas and hooded sweatshirts standing outside. One was flicking his tongue while the other had his pressed against the glass. Somerset recognized them from the boombox crowd who hung out in front of his building. He didn't know if they recognized him because it was Tracy they were leering at. He pulled out his shield and held it up to the window. The punks stepped back and scowled. One gave him the finger while the other spit on the glass. They moved on, laughing like hyenas.

"Urban youth," Somerset muttered in disgust.

Tracy tried to smile. "Perfect example. You can see why I'm nervous."

"You have to put blinders on sometimes, Tracy. Most times."

She took a sip of her coffee. Her hand was shaking. "I don't know why I asked you to come."

Somerset stirred his coffee. He had a pretty good idea why she'd called him. "Talk to him about it." he said. "He'll understand if you tell him how you feel."

"I can't be a burden, especially now," she said. "I know I'll get used to things here eventually. I guess I called you because I wanted to know what someone who's lived here thinks. Back in Springfield, it was a completely different environment. I have no perspective." She paused and took a sip. "I don't know if David told you, but I teach fifth grade . . . or did."

"He did mention it."

Suddenly Tracy was on the verge of tears, her bottom lip quivering. "I've been going around to some of the schools, looking for work, but the conditions here are . . . horrible."

"Have you tried any of the private schools?"

She shook her head and wiped her eyes with a paper napkin. "I don't know . . ."

"Tracy?" He waited until she looked him in the eye. "What's *really* bothering you?"

Her lip started to tremble again. "David and I are . . . we're going to have a baby."

Somerset sat back, relieved. He'd been certain that she was going to say they were getting divorced. He was happy for her, for both of them. But after he thought about it for a moment, he was also sad. Bringing a child into the world was something he had always denied himself. Maybe it would have saved his marriages, but he just couldn't see it, not in the city. The city turned kids into punks and petty criminals, sometimes worse.

"Tracy, I have to tell you . . . I'm not the one to talk to about this."

"I hate this city," she said.

He took out a cigarette and was about to stick it between his lips, but then he looked at Tracy's body and thought better of it. She wasn't showing yet, but the baby didn't need his secondhand smoke. He glanced out the window, still wondering why she had told *him* this. Was she thinking of aborting it? Was that it?

"Tracy, if you're thinking..." He let out a long breath and changed course. "I was married twice," he said. "Michelle—she was the first one—she was going to have our child. This was a long time ago. We had made the choice together...whether to keep the baby." He looked down into his coffee, avoiding her gaze. "Well, I got up one morning and went to work. It was just like any other day, except it was the first time since hearing about the baby. And I...I felt this strange fear. It was the first time I ever felt that way. I thought to myself, 'How can I raise a child surrounded by all this? How in God's name can a child grow up here?' So I went home, and I told Michelle I didn't want to have it. Over the next few weeks I browbeat her. I convinced her that it was wrong to have a child here. Little by little, I wore her down..."

"But I *want* to have children, William."

There was a lump in his throat. "All I can tell you, Tracy, is that I'm still positive that I made the right decision. I know it. I've seen too many kids go bad here. But there's never a day that passes that I don't wish to God that I had decided differently." He reached across the table and took her hand. "If you...don't keep the baby, if that's what you decide, then never tell David you were pregnant. I mean that. Never. I guarantee that if you do, your relationship will wither and die."

Tracy nodded, tears welling in her eyes.

He tried to smile for her. "But if you do decide to have the baby, then at that very moment when you're absolutely sure, tell David. Tell him at that exact second, and then when the baby comes, spoil that kid every single chance you get." He wiped his eyes. "That's all the advice I can give you."

"William—"

At that moment his beeper went off. He pulled it out of his pocket and checked the number on the LCD readout. It was his work number at the precinct. Actually Mills's number now.

"Excuse me. I'll be right back." He slid out of the booth and found the pay phone on the wall between the men's room and the women's room. He dropped a quarter into the slot and punched out the number. It hardly rang once.

"Detective Mills," Mills said.

"It's me. You just beeped me?"

"Yeah. Where the hell are you? I thought we were going to check out that leather shop first thing."

"We are." He flipped his wrist over and checked his watch. "I'll meet you there at nine."

"Hey, you okay?" Mills asked. "You sound funny."

Somerset coughed and sniffed. "Getting a cold, I think."

"Oh."

"I'll see you later."

"Right."

Somerset hung up the phone and went back out into the coffee shop. Tracy flashed a smile for him as he came back to the booth. "Thank you for listening," she said.

He dug into his pocket for a few dollars and dropped them on the table. "I have to run, Tracy. Work."

She grabbed his hand before he could leave. "Prom-

ise me that you'll keep in touch after you leave.
Please?"

"Sure. I promise." He nodded, then waved good-bye
and headed for the door. He couldn't say any more. The
lump in his throat was too big.

NINETEEN

Wild Bill's Leather Shop was next door to the Hog Shop, the local Harley-Davidson dealer, and Wild Bill catered to the biker crowd. His numerous wares hung from the walls and ceiling, giving the small store a certain jungle atmosphere. There were thick leather belts and wrist bands with rows of silver studs; leather vests with biker insignias on the back; biker jackets; fringed chaps; full-length leather dusters; heavy, square-toe boots; peaked caps and leather cowboy hats; leather bullwhips, and even a few customized riding crops with rhinestone handles and burred tips. The only thing pleasant about Wild Bill's shop was the smell of leather.

Somerset stood in front of the glass case by the cash register, Mills next to him, Wild Bill behind the counter. Wild Bill looked like the original rat fink, big hairy gut hanging out of an open leather vest, jagged teeth, frizzy gray hair tied back in a half-assed ponytail, multiple tattoos running up and down both arms. He was the kind of guy who gave poor white trash a bad name.

"And you say he picked it up last night?" Mills asked. "You're sure about that."

"Yup. That ain't the kind of thing you forget." He nodded down at the Polaroid photo on the counter and smiled around a mouthful of broken, yellowed teeth.

Somerset avoided looking at the photo again. It turned his stomach. Who could dream up such a horrible thing? All he could think of was somebody using it on Tracy. Ever since his conversation with her that morning, that was all he could think about, somebody hurting Tracy, hurting the baby. He glanced at Mills, feeling a little strange that he knew about the baby before Mills did.

Mills pulled out the line drawing of John Doe done by the police sketch artist. "Is this him?"

Wild Bill took the sketch and nodded thoughtfully as he studied it. "Yeah, John Doe," he said. "Easy name to remember. I figured he must be one of those performance artists. That's what I figured when he told me what he wanted. You know, one of those guys who gets up on stage, pees in a cup, and then drinks it. Performance art. One of those kind of guys." He picked up the Polaroid and admired his work. "I think I undercharged him, though. This came out nicer than I thought it would. What do you think?" He held it up for Mills to see.

Mills brushed it aside. "Gimme a break, will you?"

Wild Bill was insulted. "That's handcrafted workmanship. Not everybody can do this kind of thing."

"You're proud of that, aren't you?" Somerset said.

"Damn right, I am. I know what you're thinking, but believe me, this ain't the weirdest thing I've ever been asked to make. I've done a lot worse than this. But if that's what the customer wants . . ." Wild Bill shrugged as if it were out of his hands.

Somerset wondered if he'd be so cavalier if someone tried to use one of his creations on him.

"Did John Doe say what he was going to be using this for?" Mills asked. "Did he say anything at all like that?"

"No, he didn't say much—"

The scream of a siren outside stopped Wild Bill in the middle of his thought, his eyes wide and a little panicked. Apparently he'd had some unpleasant experiences with police in the past. A cruiser pulled up to the curb outside the shop, siren blasting, bubble lights twirling. A uniform jumped out of the passenger side and ran to the door. He opened it and stood in the doorway with his hand on the knob.

"Lieutenant," he said, looking at Somerset, "we've got another one."

Somerset instantly felt deflated, flattened by the news. But he wasn't surprised. He knew this was going to happen again. He snatched the Polaroid out of Wild Bill's hand and headed for the door. "We'll be back to talk to you some more later."

"Hey, my picture! That's the only one I've got."

"Lucky you," Somerset said as he rushed out, Mills right behind him.

"Fucking pigs!" Wild Bill grumbled behind their backs.

The outside of the Hot House Massage Parlor was painted lipstick red—door, bricks, riot gate, everything—but since it was wedged into a whole block of gaudy, neon-lit porno theaters, it didn't really stand out that much. Cruisers were parked haphazardly out front, bubble lights flashing in and out of sync. Uniforms were doing their best to keep things under control, but they weren't having an easy time of it. A steady stream of men, women, and transvestites were being escorted out of the Hot House and into a waiting police van while a crowd of local denizens jeered and shouted, shaking their fists and spitting at the cops. It was like the scumbag French Revolution.

Mills moved sideways through the crush, working his way inside with Somerset right behind him. Just inside the door, a Plexiglas ticket booth reinforced with steel bars stood guard over a lipstick-red metal door with an electronic lock that was controlled from inside the booth. The door was propped open, but the bald, fat man inside wouldn't get out of his cage. A uniform was pounding on the Plexiglas with his nightstick, losing his patience with the rat-faced fat man. Mills half-seriously wondered if he could be related to Wild Bill. There was a vague rodent resemblance.

The uniform banged on the glass again. "I said get out of the fucking booth, mister! Now!"

"Just wait!" the man grunted. "I'll come out! Just wait! When you get things under control, I'll come out."

Another uniform was trying to get a statement out of him through the glass. "Let me talk to him for while," he said to the cop with the nightstick as he bent his head to the perforated sound holes. "Did you hear any screams? Did you see anything, anything that seemed strange to you?"

"No," he croaked abruptly. The fat man sat there with his arms crossed, like a big fat bullfrog on a lily pad.

"You notice anybody coming in with a package under his arm?"

The bullfrog snorted. "Everybody who comes in here has a package under his arm. Some guys bring in suitcases full of stuff. And screams? They're screaming all the time back there. It comes with the territory, little boy."

The interrogating cop sneered at him. "You like what you do for a living, pal? You like the things you see?"

A crooked smile split the man's face. "No. I don't. But that's life, right?"

Mills and Somerset squeezed through the metal door as a middle-aged man in a black-leather corset was being led out. If he'd had a suit on, he would have looked as respectable as a banker.

Inside, the hallway walls were painted red, and naked red lightbulbs in the ceiling made it even redder. The deafening thump of heavy-metal rock music buffeted Mills's ears. The drawing of Dante's hell on the cover of his paperback version of *The Inferno* was stuck in his mind.

"Detectives?" A flustered cop in a sweat-drenched short-sleeve shirt waved to them from down the hall. "This way."

The cop led them through the labyrinth of blindingly red corridors to a room where a strobe light flashed from the ceiling. There was no other light in the room, except for the red light that spilled in from the hallway. The sweaty cop stopped at the doorway. "The suspect is under control, finally. But I don't want to go in there again. You need me, I'll be right here."

Mills stepped carefully into the room, disoriented by the strobe light. The music was just as loud in there. Two EMS workers were huddled around the suspect, a naked man—wiry, dark gray hair, about fifty-five years old—with a sheet draped over his groin. He was hand-cuffed behind his back, and he was frantic. One of the EMS workers was struggling to hold his head still while the other tried to shine a light in his pupils.

On the king-size bed in the middle of the room, the contorted form of a body lay under a sheet that had a large circular bloodstain the size of a pizza. Some of the victim's long blonde hair spilled out from the edge of the sheet. For some reason it reminded Mills of Tracy's hair, and that made him angry. Why should anything in this pigsty remind him of his wife?

"H-h-he made me do it!" the naked man stammered, struggling to get free.

"Settle down, pal!" the EMS worker with the flash-light snapped at him. "I have to look at you. This is for your own good, asshole."

On the wall over the bed, the word LUST was scratched into the red paint. Mills's hands were shaking, he was so angry when he saw it. He wanted to kick something as he went toward the bed to check out the victim.

"You're not going to want to see that more than once," the other EMS worker warned him.

"He had a gun!" the naked man screamed. "He made me do it!"

Somerset was already looking under the sheet, wincing at what he saw. Mills looked over his shoul-der, confused at first. The dead woman's upper torso was unmarked, no cuts or bruises on the face . . . But then he moved closer and saw her groin, and his stomach turned inside out. Somerset replaced the sheet.

"That was the socket," the EMS worker with the flashlight said. "Now get a load of the plug."

He pulled the sheet off the naked man. Attached to his groin was an elaborate leather contraption, a strap-on dildo with the blade of a butcher's knife sticking out of the end. The stitches on the stubby leather phallus that held the knife reminded Mills of what was left of a severed limb. The blade had dried blood on it. Wide leather straps ran around the man's waist and under his thighs. They were buckled tight, cutting into his flesh, to keep the goddamn thing on secure.

Somerset pulled out the Polaroid he'd taken from the leather shop. It was the same killer dildo, Wild Bill's masterpiece.

The first EMS guy was filling a hypodermic needle by the light of the flashlight. "We didn't want to take it off him until Forensics got here. They always get pissed off whenever we touch evidence."

"Take this thing off me," the naked man pleaded. "Take it off! Please!"

The EMS guy with the needle waved the sweaty cop back into the room to help hold the naked man still while he administered a sedative.

"Get it off! Oh, God, please! Please!"

Mills couldn't take anymore. He quickly pulled on a pair of latex gloves and hunkered down next to the man. "Hold him still," he ordered the cop. "I'll take responsibility if anybody from Forensics squawks." He started to undo the buckles, but they were pulled so tight, it pinched the man's skin to free him. When he finally got it off, angry red grooves outlined the place where the contraption had been. Mills felt the heft of the ugly thing in his hands. It was brutal and heavy, and he didn't like holding it. He placed it on the foot of the bed next to the victim.

The man's body started to relax under the uniform's hold, but he was fighting the sedative, blinking and moving his lips, struggling to get the words out. "H-h-he said . . . h-h-he asked me if I was married. He had a gun in his h-h-hand."

Somerset moved closer, hunkering down so the man could see his face. "Where was the girl?"

"The girl? W-w-what do you mean?"

"Where was the prostitute? Where was she?"

"S-s-she was on the bed. She was s-s-sitting on the bed."

"Who tied her down?" Somerset asked. "You or him?"

"He had a gun!" the man wailed. "He had a gun! He *made* it happen. He *made* me do it." The man started to sob, curling into himself. "He made me put that . . . that thing on. Oh, Christ! H-h-he made me wear it, and . . . and he told me to fuck her. He had the gun in my mouth." The man slumped forward into his own lap as the cop and the EMS worker finally let go of him. "The gun was down my fucking throat!" he cried.

Mills felt like throwing up. He remembered the taste of Doe's gun in his own mouth after Doe had bashed him in the face in the alley. He turned away and faced the bed. LUST was staring him in the face. He took his notepad out and flipped to the page where he'd written down the seven deadly sins.

Another one down, he thought, his shaking hands rattling the page. Another one to cross out. Three to go. Envy, wrath, and pride. Fuck!

SEVEN

He stared down at the spreading bloodstain and the killer dildo.

What next? he thought, infuriated and disgusted. Holy God, what next?

TWENTY

A sports bar wasn't Somerset's idea of a good watering hole, but after the day he and Mills had, a place with a lot of people and activity seemed preferable to the gloomy haunts he usually patronized. The Winner's Circle Saloon was bigger than a supermarket with all kinds of games to play—courts to shoot baskets and hockey pucks, indoor batting cages, pool tables, dart boards, even a sumo pit where people put on inflatable suits and crashed into each other until someone toppled over, helpless as a turtle on its back. Every inch of wall space was decorated with trophies, plaques, ribbons, and pennants. Somerset and Mills sat at the bar, a pitcher of beer in front of them.

Somerset sipped from a frosted mug. "My old man would come home and read me these morbid crime stories," he said. " 'The Murders in the Rue Morgue,' 'Le Fanu's Green Tea,' stuff like that. My mother would give him hell because he was keeping me up till all hours." .

Mills was hunched over his beer. "Sounds like a father who wanted his son to follow in his footsteps."

Somerset suddenly wondered if Mills knew that he knew Tracy was pregnant. But how would he know? They'd been together all day, and Tracy wouldn't have told him over the phone. Mills couldn't have known.

Somerset set down his mug on the bar. "One birthday my father gave me my first brand-new hardcover book, *The Century of the Detective* by Jurgen Thorwald. It traced the history of deduction as a science, and it sealed my fate because it was real, not fiction. That a drop of blood or a piece of hair could solve a crime—that was incredible to me." He poured more beer into Mills's mug, then topped off his own. He could sense that Mills was tied up in knots over this John Doe business, and he wanted him to relax, to put this whole thing into perspective before he drove himself nuts. "You know, there's not going to be a happy ending to this. It's not possible."

"If we just get him, I'll be happy enough," Mills said.

"No. Stop thinking of it as good versus evil. That's not how it is."

"How the hell can you say that? Especially after today?"

"Listen. A man beats his wife to a pulp, or, say, a wife shoots her husband. We wash the blood off the walls, put the killer in jail, but in the end who won? Tell me."

"You do your job—"

"But there's no victory in it," Somerset insisted.

Mills picked up his mug. "You follow the law and do the best you can. That's all you can do."

"If we catch John Doe, and he is the devil, if he actually is Satan himself, that might live up to our expectations. But he's not the devil. He's just a man."

Mills was glaring at him. "Why don't you just shut up for a while? You bitch and complain about everything. What? Do you think you're preparing me for hard times? You're not. You're leaving. I'm the one who's staying here to fight the fight."

A photo of a young Muhammad Ali over the bar caught Somerset's eye. "But who are you fighting for? People don't want champions anymore. They just want to play Lotto and eat cheeseburgers."

"What're you trying to do, talk me out of working here? You want me to run away to the sticks with you?"

Yes, Somerset thought. *For the sake of your baby.*

"Christ, Lieutenant, I may be out of line here, but how the hell did you end up like this? Huh?"

Somerset took a sip and thought about it. "It wasn't one thing in particular that turned my head around if that's what you mean. It's just that . . . I just can't live where apathy is embraced and nurtured as if it were a virtue. I can't take that anymore."

"Which means you're better than everyone else, right? Because you've got higher standards."

Somerset shook his head. "Wrong. My problem is that I sympathize completely with everybody's situation. Too completely. But apathy is the one thing I can't accept. Unfortunately it's also the one thing that really works in places like this. Think about it. It's so much easier to lose yourself in drugs than to cope with life. Easier to steal something than to earn it. Easier to beat a child than to raise it because it takes *so much* work to love, to care."

"You're talking about people who are mentally ill, people who—"

"No, I'm not. I'm talking about everyday life, normal people who are just trying to get by, people like you and me. You can't afford to be this naive, Mills."

Mills slammed his mug down on the bar. "Fuck you! Listen to yourself. You're telling me the problem with people is they don't care, so *you* can't care either. That's bullshit, man. It doesn't make any sense, and you wanna know why—"

"But do *you* care?" Somerset interrupted.

"Damn right I do."

"And you, David Mills, are going to make a difference?"

Mills turned in his seat and got in Somerset's face. "Yeah, I am. 'Naive' as that may sound to you. And you wanna know what? I don't think you're quitting because you believe the things you're saying. I think you *want* to believe them because it makes you feel better. It makes you feel justified. You *want* me to agree with you. 'Yeah, you're absolutely right, Lieutenant. This is fucked. Let's go live in a fucking log cabin in the woods.' Well, I *don't* agree with you. I can't afford to because I'm staying." Mills got up off his stool and threw some money on the bar. "Thanks for the beer." He stomped off, heading for the door.

Two beer-bellied white guys in warm-up jackets and baseball caps down at the end of the bar were staring at him. Somerset didn't realize that they'd been yelling. The bartender was staring, too. Somerset took out a cigarette and fumbled with his lighter, but the damn thing wouldn't catch. Finally it did, but his hand was trembling as he tried to hold the flame steady. *Goddamn hard-headed son of a bitch!* he thought. Mills was going to fuck up his life but good. Not only his life, Tracy's and the baby's, too. Mills was going down the same senseless road he had taken, the stupid ass.

Somerset tried to lift his mug, but his hands wouldn't stop shaking. Mentally he could hear the steady beat of his metronome as he tried to calm himself the way he did at home. Tick . . . tick . . . tick . . . But it didn't help. This place was too noisy, people playing all these games, guys arguing over sports, guys trying to pick up women, women playing games with the men, people fooling themselves, playing games they thought they could win.

He picked up his mug and wandered over to the dart board court at the far side of the bar. He stared at one of the targets, concentrating on it, trying to block out everything but the metronome in his head.

Tick . . . tick . . . tick . . .

He tossed at the board, paying less attention to his aim than to the rhythm, picking up his pace until it matched the ticking in his head—a *thwack* into the target for every tick of the metronome. Tick, *thwack* . . . tick, *thwack* . . . tick, *thwack* . . . Somerset kept throwing, not thinking, just throwing. Tick, *thwack* . . . tick, *thwack* . . . tick, *thwack* . . .

"Hey, mister," the bartender said. He was leaning over the end of the bar, and he looked a little nervous.

"What?" Somerset's brow was beaded with sweat. He didn't want to be bothered right now.

"Think you could use darts instead of . . ." The bartender nodded toward the dartboard.

Somerset's switchblade was embedded in the cork just south of the bull's eye.

SEVEN

Jesus! he thought, quickly pulling it out and putting it away. He hadn't even realized that he'd taken it out. He clutched the mother-of-pearl handle in his pocket. His hands were still shaking.

TWENTY-ONE

Mills's head was throbbing when he got home that night but not because of the beer. Moving as quietly as he could through his darkened living room, he was still pissed off at Somerset and all his goddamn lecturing. If Somerset had all the goddamn answers, why was he such a sad case himself? Where the hell did he get off telling other people how to run their lives when his own was such a mess? What kind of person just runs away from his problems? Someone who can't face them, that's who. So he was no one to talk.

Mills felt his way to the dining room table where the streetlights outside threw a dim light into the room. He pulled out one of the chairs, sat down, and started to take off his shoes. Mojo, the golden retriever, sidled up to his leg, looking for a head scratch. Mills obliged, ruffling the dog's ears, but Mojo didn't respond with the usual tongue-flapping tail-wag. The dog seemed depressed, Mills thought. Or maybe just tired.

Mills left his shoes under the chair and went to the bedroom, stepping lightly in his stocking feet, wishing the apartment's wood floors weren't so squeaky. He took off his clothes, careful not to wake Tracy, laying them on a chair. He pulled down his underpants and kicked them off before he eased under the covers, snuggling up to Tracy's body, feeling her warmth against his skin. Shrugging the covers up over his shoulders, he probed with his face until he found hers, kissing first her forehead, then her cheek. He didn't want to wake her, but he did want her to wake up. Thanks to goddamn Somerset, he was too wound up to fall asleep. He snaked his arm under her head and hugged her, kissing her face again.

"Honey . . . ?" she moaned, still half asleep.

"Ssshhh," he said, running his fingers along her cheek. "Go back to sleep."

"What's wrong?" she said.

"Nothing . . ." He stared at the silhouette of her profile. "I love you."

She moaned and turned over, pulling him tight.

Mills closed his eyes, telling himself that he could never end up like Somerset because he had Tracy. If Somerset had had a Tracy, he wouldn't have turned out the way he did. The guy may be a fucking know-it-all, but he didn't have a Tracy. Only he, fucking David Mills, had a Tracy. . . .

Mills soon fell asleep, he and his wife clinging onto each another.

The first ring of the phone hit him like a sledgehammer. Mills sat up, his heart pounding.

From the foot of the bed, Mojo barked and Lucky growled.

Tracy's nails were digging into his forearm. "David! What is it?"

Mills reached over and snatched the receiver before it rang again. "Hello!"

"*I've gone and done it again.*"

His blood turned to ice. He felt unclean just holding the receiver to his face. He knew that whiny voice. It was John Doe. How the hell did he get this number? Mills looked over at Tracy. His heart was slamming.

"Doe? Doe! Are you there? Talk to me!"

"It's not Doe, it's me." Somerset's voice came on the line. "That was a recording."

Mills was instantly infuriated. "What the fuck is wrong with you, Somerset?" He looked at the clock radio on Tracy's side of the bed. It was 4:38 in the morning.

"I got a call about twenty minutes ago from the uniform guarding Doe's apartment. Doe called his own phone and left that message. We'd rigged his phone just in case."

Mills threw back the covers, cradling his head. He was groggy as hell. Too much beer and not enough sleep. "Is that all he said?"

"Yes. We also found another body. Pride."

"Oh, shit . . ."

Tracy was up on her elbows. She looked worried and anxious.

"Look, Mills, you want to fight this fight, I'll fight it with you. Just get your ass down here right now."

"Hey, don't do me any fucking favors, Som—"

"Seventeen-hundred Basin Avenue, apartment 5G."

"Wait a minute—"

But Somerset had already hung up.

"David," Tracy said, "what's going on?" There was panic in her voice.

SEVEN

Mills hobbled to the bathroom. "I wish I knew," he grumbled. "I wish I knew."

When Mills arrived at 1700 Basin Avenue, apartment 5G, the forensics people were already in motion. One guy was down on his hands and knees, searching for hairs and fibers in the aqua-blue, wall-to-wall living room carpet.

A female technician was in the bathroom, checking out the contents of the medicine cabinet. Mills noticed that there were about two inches of standing water in the tub. It was pinkish. Tinged with blood, he assumed.

Dear little Smudge was in the kitchen, dusting the knife rack for prints.

"Morning," Mills said to her.

"Fuck you." She didn't even look up from her work.

"Where's Somerset?"

"Fu—"

"Never mind. I'll find him myself." *Great way to start the day*, Mills thought.

He went down a short hallway and found Somerset in the bedroom. Dr. O'Neill, the city medical examiner, was with him. The room was decorated like a valentine—all pink and red with lace trim. The first thing that caught Mills's eye were the words scrawled in scarlet lipstick on the Pepto-Bismol-pink wall over the bed: PRIDE—then in smaller letters underneath—I DID NOT KILL HER. SHE WAS GIVEN A CHOICE.

Sitting up in bed was the corpse, a floral-print comforter neatly folded back just under her breasts. She was wearing a white lace peignoir. Her face was sloppily bandaged with gauze and tape, crude openings left for her eyes and mouth. Blood spots stained the gauze dead center in the middle of her face. The bed was crowded with dozens of stuffed animals. A white unicorn was in her lap. Mills picked up the unicorn and examined it, then put it back in her lap.

The victim's arms were outside the covers. In her right hand she was holding a cordless telephone; in her left a brown plastic prescription bottle. She was holding the bottle upside down. Two red pills had spilled out onto the comforter.

"Sleeping pills," Somerset said. "The bottle's glued to her hand. So's the phone. He apparently used superglue."

Dr. O'Neill leaned over the corpse with a pair of surgical scissors and carefully started to cut through the bandages around her head. Mills stared at her masked face, his heart pounding, dreading what he was going to see.

Somerset tapped him on the shoulder. "I found this in her purse." He showed Mills the woman's driver's license. The photo of her was absolutely stunning. Long raven hair and dazzling sapphire eyes. Her name was Linda Abernathy, age twenty-eight. She could easily have been a fashion model.

The doctor was peeling back the gauze. Mills started wincing before he even saw it, then his stomach bottomed out. The woman's nose was gone. Patches of bone peeked through the severed tissue. Mills had to look away.

"He cut her up, then dressed the wounds," Somerset said. He picked up the hand glued to the phone. " 'Call for help, and you'll live,' he must have told her. '*But* you'll be disfigured.' " He pointed to the hand holding the pill bottle. "Or else just put yourself out of your misery."

Dr. O'Neill lifted her head and removed the rest of the bandaging. "He cut off her nose—"

"To spite her face," Somerset finished.

"And he did it fairly recently," the doctor added. "There isn't much clotting in these wounds."

Mills looked at her face again, but that was a mistake. Her eyes seemed alive. He left the room quickly, going through the living room and out into the hallway. He needed some air.

Twenty minutes later Mills and Somerset were driving back to the precinct house in Mills's car. Downtown traffic was crawling. They were right in the middle of morning rush hour.

Mills was on edge, but not just because of the traffic. He'd seen hundreds of corpses in his career, but never once had he ever been squeamish, even when he was a rookie. But this one got to him. And worst of all, it happened in front of Somerset.

He glanced over at the lieutenant who was deep in thought, smoking a cigarette as he stared out the side window. Linda Abernathy's face apparently hadn't bothered Somerset. Of course Somerset was the guy who'd taught himself not to care anymore, Mills thought. He was the hard-ass city dweller. Nothing bothered him because he didn't let it bother him.

Mills tapped on the steering wheel impatiently. The traffic light up ahead had just turned red again. This was the third time he'd seen it turn, and they'd hardly moved. The car behind him was revving its engine. Mills looked in the side mirror. It was a cabbie acting like an asshole. He glanced over at Somerset again, leisurely smoking as if he had all the time in the world.

"Didn't that bother you back there?" Mills finally had to ask.

Somerset just nodded, still staring out the window.

"What're you, meditating for Chrissake? Say something. I don't know about you, but I'm pissed at shit. This has to stop. Doe is going down. I don't care how I have to do it, but he's going down."

Somerset took another long drag. He didn't seem to be listening. "I've decided to stay until this is over. Till it's either done, or it becomes obvious that it's never going to finish."

"Oh, really." Mills was glaring at him. "Is this for my benefit? You don't think I can handle it alone?"

Somerset looked at him sideways. "One of two things will happen. Either we're going to get John Doe, or he'll finish his series of seven, and this case will go on for years."

"So what's that got to do with you and your retirement? You think you're doing me a big favor by staying? I told you last night, you're not." The light turned red again. They'd only moved a single car length at the most, and the precinct house was only around the corner. Mills looked in the rearview mirror. The yellow cab was inching up his ass, revving the engine, as if that would get things moving.

"I'm requesting that you keep me on as your partner for a few more days," Somerset said. "You'd be doing *me* a favor."

Mills had to laugh. "What am I going to say? No?"

"You could."

"Yeah, right." Mills had had enough of this traffic.

He reached under the seat for the small blue bubble light and set it on top of the dashboard. He hit the siren and started the light, inching up on the guy in front of him.

"As soon as this is over, I'm gone," Somerset said.

"What a big surprise. You can't fucking wait to get out of here. Why don't you just go now?"

"Can't leave this unfinished . . . Can't leave any loose ends."

"Yeah, right." Mills cut the wheel sharply to the right and got behind a city bus in a bus stop. He worked the wah-wah on the siren, hounding the bus to pull out into the intersection as soon as the light turned green. If the bus made it through, he could follow in its wake and make the turn. Mills didn't let up on the siren, and the bus driver picked up on his cue, slipping into the intersection just before the light turned. Angry horns honked as it blocked the rest of the traffic, but Mills had just enough room to get around the corner. The pain-in-the-ass cab stayed right on his tail and made the turn right after him.

Police cars were parked at an angle on the entire side of the street where the precinct house stood. Mills found an empty spot and pulled up to the curb. The cab drove on to the front door of the precinct and stopped there, letting out some little slob whose shirt was hanging out of his pants. The angry drivers behind the cab honked and cursed, but Mills paid them no mind.

Somerset and Mills got out of the car and headed up the front steps into the precinct. Mills pushed through the front doors and went in first. Uniforms and plainclothes cops were going about their business as the day shift was about to go on duty. Mills went directly to the duty sergeant standing over the large battered duty desk just inside the front doors. "Mills and Somerset are on the premises," he said to the sergeant.

"Fucking wonderful," the sergeant snarled.

California was standing behind the desk with the duty sergeant, sorting through a fistful of message slips. He pulled out a pack and handed them to Mills. "Your wife just called," he said. "Do us a favor and get yourself an answering machine, will ya, Mills?"

Asshole, Mills thought as he took the message slips. He held his tongue, though, and quickly looked through his messages instead. Stuffing the slips into his pocket, he went to catch up with Somerset who was already halfway up the stairs.

"Excuse me. Detective?"

Mills kept walking.

"Detective?"

The insistent voice stopped Mills in his tracks. He turned around and nearly shit his pants. It was John Doe. He was the little slob who'd just gotten out of that cab. Holy shit!

Doe flashed a shy smile and shrugged, palms up, as if to say, "Here I am." His shirt and pants were soaked with blood.

"Jesus . . ." This was unreal. Mills couldn't believe this was happening.

"It's him!" California suddenly shouted from behind the duty desk. He pulled his gun and vaulted over the desk. "It's Doe!" He raced up to Doe and stuck the barrel of his gun in Doe's ear. "On the ground, asshole! Arms out! Move!"

By this time, Mills and several other cops had their weapons out, all trained on John Doe who was down on his knees, looking up imploringly at Mills.

"Get down!" Mills shouted. "Face down on the floor!"

California prodded Doe with his gun. "You heard him, fuckface! Get down!"

"Be careful!" Somerset yelled, coming back down the stairs.

Doe was down on his stomach, doing what he was told, but Mills wasn't taking any chances. He moved in and straddled the bastard, putting his gun dead center at the base of his neck. "Spread your legs and put your hands behind your head!"

Doe obeyed without hesitation.

"Now don't move!" Mills shouted. "Don't move one fucking inch!"

Other cops swarmed over Doe's prone body. One got a pair of cuffs on him. Two others started frisking him.

Somerset squeezed in, getting down on one knee. "I don't believe this," he murmured. He stared at Doe's handcuffed hands at the small of his back. Every bloody finger was wrapped and re-wrapped with Band-Aids.

John Doe turned his head to the side and smiled at Somerset. "Hello."

"Shut up!" California yelled. He leaned on his gun and pressed Doe's face into the floor, twisting his glasses askew.

"Stand him up and read him his rights," Somerset ordered.

Two uniforms hauled Doe up by the armpits, and California started to recite the Miranda rights, enunciating it loud and clear, right in his face. "You have the right to remain silent. You have the right to . . ."

Mills whispered to Somerset. "What the fuck is this? I don't get it."

Somerset could only shake his head.

When California finished reading John Doe his rights, Doe looked to Mills again. "I want to speak to my lawyer."

TWENTY-TWO

Forty-five minutes later Somerset was staring into one of the precinct's stark interrogation rooms through a one-way mirror. Inside, John Doe was hand-cuffed to a table that was bolted to the floor, calmly looking around the room, sitting there as if he were waiting for a bus. He looked like an eccentric college professor, a physicist, something like that. He wasn't raving, he wasn't angry, he wasn't howling at the moon. There was a casual, almost lazy look to his eyes.

His lawyer, Mark Swarr, was sitting across the table, apparently asking him questions, taking notes on a legal pad. The mike was turned off, so Somerset couldn't hear what they were saying. He would have loved to hear what they were saying, but he couldn't listen in. Attorney-client privilege. It would be an infringement of Doe's rights, the kind of technicality that could get Doe's case thrown out of court.

This had to go by the book, Somerset thought to himself. Doe could not walk. He could not have his freedom ever again. Not for a minute.

Somerset's eyes narrowed as he studied the lawyer,

wondering why Doe had chosen him. Swarr was about thirty or so, dark suit, white shirt, dark curly hair, bad posture. He was just two years out of Legal Aid and into his own practice, an eager beaver out to make it on his own. What he notably lacked was the requisite killer instinct that the seasoned criminal attorneys had. Swarr had represented his share of low-level drug dealers, but so far none of the heavy hitters had used him. Somerset doubted that he'd ever make it to the ranks of high-priced suits and mob mouthpieces who did legal cartwheels for their criminal clients and pulled down big bucks for their stunts. But this was what Somerset couldn't figure out. If Doe could afford his own lawyer, why didn't he get himself a top-notch big mouth? Why Swarr? Swarr was only slightly better than the freebie lawyers from Legal Aid.

The door behind Somerset opened, and Mills and the captain walked into the observation room. Somerset could see their reflection in the glass. Mills went directly to the mirror, fixing his gaze on Doe. The captain handed Somerset a fingerprint card, the black ink prints smeared and mingled with blood.

"Useless," the captain said with a disgusted snort. "Doe apparently cuts off the skin on his fingertips on a regular basis. That's why we couldn't find a single usable print in his apartment. He admitted that he's been doing this for quite a while. He said he knows what he's doing, that he cuts them before the papillary line can grow back." The captain took the card back and ripped it in half.

"What about the trace on his bank account?" Mills asked. "And the guns we found at his apartment? The guy has to have a past. There must be something that connects him to it."

"So far it's all been dead ends," the captain said. "No credit history. No employment records. His bank account is only five years old, and every transaction has been in cash. We're even trying to trace his furniture to see if he came here from someplace else. But for now all we know is that he's independently wealthy, seems to be well-educated, and is totally insane. And we may never know how he got this way."

"He's John Doe by choice," Somerset said, staring through the glass at him. "He's his own creation. Dr. Frankenstein and the monster all in one."

"When do we get to question him, Captain?" Mills asked.

"You don't."

"What?"

"Because he's confessing, it goes straight to the prosecutor's office."

Mills ran his fingers through his hair. "He wouldn't just turn himself in. It doesn't make any sense. He doesn't have any remorse. Just look at him."

"Maybe it's not supposed to make any sense," the captain said. "I give up. I don't know."

Somerset lit a cigarette. "He's not finished yet."

The captain laughed. "What's he going to do from a jail cell?"

Somerset squinted against the drifting smoke. "I don't know, but I do know he's not finished yet. He can't be."

"He's pissing in our faces, that's what he's doing," Mills shouted. "And we're just fucking taking it!"

The captain just stared at him for a moment. "You

want some advice, Mills? Let it go. You're wound too tight. It's up to the prosecutor's office now. So just let it go. And that's not an option. You understand what I'm saying?" The captain tossed the torn print card into the trash on his way out.

Mills put his forehead to the glass and pressed his fingers against it one by one, cracking his knuckles.

Somerset could see that the captain was right. Mills definitely was wound too tight. But what Somerset didn't know was how tight. How far would Mills go to get back at Doe?

Mills started to crack the knuckles on his other hand. "You know he's fucking with us," he said.

Somerset let out a long sigh. "Probably for the first time since we've met, you and I are in total agreement. Doe just wouldn't stop like this. There's more to it."

"But what?"

"He's two murders away from finishing his master-piece. He's still got envy and wrath to go. But I can't imagine how he intends to finish it. Can you?"

"Maybe he's already finished. We just haven't found the bodies yet."

"Somehow I don't think so. This guy is big on sending out messages. Why be quiet about his last two? These should be his grand finale."

"Maybe . . ." Mills shrugged, his head still pressed to the glass.

Somerset focused on the lawyer's yellow legal pad, Mark Swarr scribbling down notes a mile a minute. "I'm afraid we'll just have to wait for Doe's plea."

Mills breathed on the glass. In the condensation, he wrote WRATH and ENVY.

In the interrogation room, John Doe had nodded off.

TWENTY-THREE

Just after one o'clock that afternoon, Somerset and Mills were summoned to the captain's office for a meeting. When they arrived, John Doe's lawyer, Mark Swarr, and District Attorney Martin Talbot were sitting in the two chairs across from the captain's desk. The captain was frowning, elbows on his desk, fingers steepled over his lips. He looked like an egg frying. The lawyers, on the other hand, looked like lawyers—nothing bothered them. Except Somerset did notice a thin line of sweat on the district attorney's upper lip. This was unusual for Talbot. His feathers didn't ruffle easily. Of course, this case was breaking new ground for everybody.

Mills and Somerset nodded to all present and found spaces for themselves in the crowded office. Mills leaned against the window sill. Somerset stayed standing, propping his elbow on a tall file cabinet.

The captain looked at Swarr as he nodded toward the detectives. "Tell them."

Swarr turned sideways in his seat to face them. "My client has informed me that there are two more bodies

. . . two more victims, hidden away. He says he'll reveal them, but only to Detectives Mills and Somerset, and only at six o'clock today."

Talbot snorted out a laugh as he pulled the burgundy silk handkerchief out of his breast pocket and blotted the sweat off his upper lip. "Christ . . ."

"Why us?" Mills asked.

Swarr shrugged. "He says he admires you."

Somerset caught the captain's eye and shook his head. "This is all part of his game. It's obvious."

It could be a bluff, Somerset thought. Or a trap. The bodies were probably real, though. Doe had to finish his masterpiece, and these two would complete the seven deadly sins. Envy and wrath.

"My client claims that if the detectives do not accept this offer, these two bodies will never be found."

"Frankly, counselor," Talbot said, stuffing his handkerchief back in his pocket, "I'm inclined to let those bodies rot."

"We don't make deals, Mr. Swarr," the captain added.

"Look," Mills said, jumping to his feet and jutting his finger into Swarr's face, "your boy's already in line to get his free room and board and cable TV courtesy of the state, just like every other scumbag killer in this state. So why don't you just be on your way, pal? He's not getting any more out of us."

"Ease back, Mills," the captain warned.

But Mills was up on his soapbox now, and he wasn't finished having his say. "How can you defend this piece of shit? How? Are you proud of yourself for doing this?"

Swarr didn't flinch. "Detective, as you know, I'm required by law to serve my clients to the best of my ability and to serve their best interests."

"Yeah, well, serve this." Mills gave him the finger as he flopped back against the window sill.

"You're pushing it, Mills!" the captain barked.

"It's all right, Captain," Swarr said. "I understand that your people have been under a lot of stress with this thing."

Mills was on his feet again. "I don't *want* you to understand my stress, asshole."

"Sit down!" the captain shouted, glowering at Mills.

Swarr turned to the district attorney. "My client also wants to inform you that if you do not accept his offer, he will plead insanity across the board."

Talbot snorted up another laugh. "Let him try." But the film of sweat had returned to his upper lip. "I'm telling you right now. I am not letting this conviction slide. No way."

"My client has also informed me that if you accept his offer, under his specific conditions, he will sign a full confession and plead guilty to all the murders right now."

The room went silent. Talbot and the captain avoided each other's glances, not wanting to let on that Swarr had just played his ace and played it well. Mills looked to Somerset, but Somerset made himself busy taking out a cigarette and lighting it. This whole thing stunk as far as he was concerned. Doe had been in control from the very beginning, and his "offer" just kept him in control. If Doe had two more victims hidden away somewhere, so what? They were already dead. Why not just let the guy stew for a while? What was the big hurry?

But Somerset could see that Mills was itching to wrap this thing up. His body language was screaming it. Big mistake. Never let the other guy see how much you want something. Somerset was disappointed in him. Mills still had a lot to learn.

The captain looked up at Mills. "What do you think?"

"Let's go for it."

Somerset took a long drag off his cigarette. *Not smart,* he thought.

Swarr twisted around and looked at Somerset. "My client has stipulated that it has to be both of you."

Somerset didn't answer right away. "If your client were to claim insanity, this conversation would be admissible. The fact that he's blackmailing us with his plea would work against him."

"Perhaps," Swarr said. "But my client wants to remind you that two more people are dead. I don't have to tell you what the press would do if they found out that the police showed little concern in regards to finding these people, so that their loved ones could give them a proper burial."

"Sounds like you've got the press release already written, Counselor," Somerset said.

"As I said, Detective, I only act in my client's best interests."

Somerset stared down at him, letting the smoke drift out of his nose. "This is all assuming that there really are two more bodies, Counselor."

Talbot looked disgruntled as he reached into his pocket for a folded piece of paper. "I got a preliminary lab report just a little while ago. They did a quickie on Doe's clothing and fingernails. They found his own blood from cutting his fingerprints off." Talbot paused and sighed. "They also found blood from Linda Abernathy, the woman whose face he disfigured . . . as well as blood from a third party . . . as yet unidentified." Talbot turned around and looked to Somerset. "You would be escorting an unarmed man."

Somerset want to spit. Talbot was folding. Somerset expected better from him.

Mills started for the door. "Come on, man. Let's finish it."

But Somerset stayed put. He crossed his arms and looked at the floor, the cigarette smoldering between his fingers. He could feel the piece of wallpaper from his new house in his shirt pocket. "As of yesterday I'm officially retired," he said. "I've got nothing to do with this anymore."

"What the fuck are you talking about?" Mills was incensed again.

"My client made it very clear," Swarr said. "It has to be Mills *and* Somerset. Not just one, and no substitutes."

All eyes were on Somerset.

The captain was doing a slow burn. He knew this was all out of whack, but Swarr had them by the balls.

Talbot's forehead was getting sweaty. No doubt he was thinking about that press conference, Swarr telling the world that the DA didn't give a shit about two dead people. Talbot's chances of running for public office would go right down the toilet if that happened.

Mills was going nuts, thinking he wouldn't get to wrap this up. He didn't realize that in real life, you seldom get a nice neat beginning, middle, and end. If it's closure you want, go read a novel.

Of course, Somerset wanted a little closure, too. He wanted to wrap up at least the major loose ends, so he could retire. If he left a lot of shit behind, Mills would be right, he'd be quitting.

Somerset took another drag off his cigarette. This wasn't the way to do it. Giving John Doe control of the situation was a mistake. In his gut, Somerset knew that.

"So what's it gonna be, William?" the captain asked.

Somerset looked from one face to the next. Mills was jumping out of his skin, waiting for him to agree to this insanity. Somerset felt the wallpaper rose in his pocket again.

"William?"

He looked at the floor and didn't answer.

Later that afternoon Somerset and Mills stood side-by-side before two adjoining sinks in the precinct locker room. They were both shirtless, both chests covered with shaving cream. An open package of disposable razors sat on the edge of Mills's sink. He studied himself in the mirror, positioning the razor in his hand, trying to get his bearings. Finally he took his first tentative stroke straight down the center of his chest.

Somerset hesitated, a cigarette burning between his lips. He still didn't like this whole setup with Doe calling all the shots. He also didn't like Mills's attitude. He was too eager. Somerset didn't know why the hell he was agreeing to this. Maybe he was too eager, too.

He caught Mills's eye in the mirror. "If John Doe's head splits open and a UFO flies out, I want you to have expected it. *Nothing* should surprise you."

Mills was positioning his hand so he could shave his right pec. "What the fuck are you talking about?"

"You'd better expect anything, my friend, because whether you choose to admit it or not, Doe is going to be in control. He's telling us where to go, when to go, and how to get there. If you're comfortable with this situation, then you're a bigger jackass than I thought."

Mills gestured toward his partially shaven chest. "What're you talking about, control? You think I'm doing this 'cause I like it? We're going to be wearing body mikes. California will be following us up in the copter. He'll hear every word we say. If Doe farts, California will be right there with a clothespin for your nose. Another thing, I don't give a shit what happens, Doe is not getting out of those cuffs. I don't care if friggin' E.T. comes out of the sky to bring his boy home, Doe does not get loose."

"Don't treat this lightly, Mills. I'm telling you."

"And don't treat me like I'm your son, for Chrissake," Mills snapped. "I am not a kid, and this is not my first case."

Somerset held his tongue when he heard that. In all the confusion, he'd forgotten about Tracy being pregnant. Mills still didn't know. *What if something went wrong?* he thought. What if Doe was setting a trap for them? What if something happened to Mills? Tracy would be a widow. She'd have to raise the child without a father.

Somerset flicked his cigarette across the room into a urinal. That settled it. Even if Doe would've allowed it, Somerset couldn't let this idiot Mills go out there by himself. He had to protect Mills. He picked up a razor and got to work on his own chest.

Mills had a finger over his nipple as he carefully shaved around it. "If I were to accidentally cut off one of my nipples, would that be covered under workman's comp?"

"I suppose so." Somerset worked his razor carefully, taking short strokes and frequently swishing off the excess shaving cream in the standing water in the sink. "If you were man enough to actually file the claim, I'd buy you a new one myself. Out of my own pocket."

Mills grinned as he worked around the other nipple. "You must really like me then."

Somerset gave him a dirty look in the mirror. "Don't push it, Mills."

TWENTY-FOUR

Mills and Somerset had moved on to the Homicide Squad bullpen to finish their preparations. The stand-up blackboard still had the seven deadly sins written on it, five of the sins crossed out. A television had been wheeled in, so they could monitor what was going on outside. The set was on, but the sound was turned down.

Somerset stared at the TV as he buttoned up his shirt. He shrugged his shoulders, trying to get comfortable with the body mike taped to his chest. The front of the precinct house was on the screen, a gang of reporters crowded around for DA Martin Talbot's announcement on the capture of John Doe. But Talbot hadn't made his entrance yet because Somerset and Mills weren't ready. They'd send down word as soon as they were. The district attorney was going to be their decoy.

After Somerset tucked his shirttails in, he went into his pants pocket for a roll of Rolaids. He popped two into his mouth and offered the roll to Mills. Mills, who was itching get going, took two and handed the roll back to Somerset. As Somerset chewed the chalky antacids, he knotted his tie, then put on a tan-colored bulletproof vest, adjusting the Velcro straps at the shoulders, so that it was snug but not too tight.

Mills already had his vest on. He was standing over a desk, feeding bullets into a clip. When he finished, he slid the clip into his nine millimeter and racked the slide, checking and double-checking his weapon.

Somerset's weapon was in its holster, hanging from the back of a chair. He shrugged into the holster, removed the gun, and checked the clip carefully. When he was satisfied that it was operable, he put the weapon away and put on his gray tweed sports jacket. He looked at Mills. "You ready?"

"Yup." Mills was fixing the collar of his leather jacket.

Somerset glanced at the TV for a second, then looked out the window. A setting orange sun was impaled on the jutting skyline. He picked up the phone and pressed the captain's number. "We're on our way down, captain," Somerset said. "Give us five minutes, then send Talbot out."

On the roof of police headquarters a mile away, a sleek black helicopter sat on the helipad, the pilot behind the controls waiting for instructions. Two police sharpshooters sat by the open bay, cradling identical rifles with high-power scopes. A steady dry wind off the desert buffeted the chopper, sending a muffled whoosh through the interior of the craft.

A lone figure in black riot gear emerged from the rooftop doorway that led into the building and trotted to the chopper, getting in next to the pilot. It was California. "We got the green light," he said to the pilot. "Start her up."

The pilot nodded and handed California a crash helmet just like the one he was wearing.

"You think this wind will hurt us?" California asked before he put it on.

The pilot shook his head. "Just makes the ride more fun." He started the engine. Through the cockpit windshield, California looked up and watched the rotors starting to turn.

In the basement parking garage of the precinct house, Somerset sat behind the wheel of an idling metallic blue, unmarked police car. Behind the wire-mesh barrier that separated the front seat from the back, Mills sat with John Doe.

Doe was wearing a khaki jumpsuit courtesy of the precinct maintenance crew. He was in handcuffs and leg irons, which were attached to each other with a second pair of handcuffs. A third pair chained Doe's left wrist to the wire-mesh barrier. Circles of sweat stained the armpits of the jumpsuit, but his expression remained placid, almost dreamy, despite his bonds.

A uniformed cop stood outside in the sunlight at the top of the ramp, a walkie-talkie in his hand. Somerset kept his eye on him, waiting for the signal to go. As soon as DA Talbot started the press conference, the uniform would get the word on the walkie-talkie.

John Doe started to hum to himself, very softly. Somerset kept his focus on the uniform. A few moments later the uniform gave them the thumbs-up.

As Somerset put the car into gear, he caught Mill's eye in the rearview mirror. Neither man said anything.

They didn't have to. Somerset pressed the accelerator, and the car moved slowly up the ramp. The uniform watched for traffic on the street, then waved them on when it was clear. Somerset picked up speed and guided the car out into daylight. Mills pressed Doe's head down, so he couldn't be seen.

Somerset turned right into the street, then drove down to the end of the block and took another right, heading for the freeway. As they went through the intersection, he glanced to the right where the mob of reporters were shouting questions at DA Talbot, waving tape recorders in the air, setting off camera flashes in his face. Somerset didn't slow down. Even though Doe was wearing a bulletproof vest, they weren't going to take any chances. The whole city was up in arms over these killings. There were plenty of angry citizens who believed in swift justice and wouldn't mind taking a potshot at the monster. Somerset wasn't so sure he wasn't one of them. John Doe certainly believed in capital punishment. So why should he be immune?

As inner city streets gave way to the wider boulevards, Somerset picked up speed. He knew he'd feel a little better once they were on the freeway and out of the city. Sweat was dripping down the small of his back. He knew the Kel transmitter taped to his chest was supposed to be waterproof, but he still worried about getting it wet. He had a feeling he was going to be doing a lot more sweating before the day was done.

Sailing down Lincoln Boulevard, Somerset suddenly frowned. There was a yellow school bus up ahead, lights flashing. Kids were filing out, mothers assembled at the curb to greet them. Fathers, too. Somerset considered not stopping and going around the bus. There were too many people around; someone could look into the car and see Doe chained up back there. Some irate father could be carrying a gun.

But what if he hit a kid going around the bus? Even a near miss would start an incident, and that would draw attention to them. Somerset started to slow down, praying that the bus would move before he had to come to a full stop. But kids were still coming off the bus, so Somerset pulled to a stop a good seventy-five feet behind it and kept his hand on the gear shift, prepared to throw it in reverse and get the hell out of there at the first sign of trouble.

He watched as parents found their children, kissed them, hugged them, relieved them of their backpacks and lunchboxes. This would be Tracy some day, Somerset thought, Mills, too, if he was smart. Mills should get involved in his kid's upbringing, be a part of the child's life in every possible way. Somerset glanced in the rearview mirror at Mills holding Doe's head down. *All Mills has to do is get through today,* Somerset thought.

The bus's lights stopped flashing, and it finally started to pull away. Somerset waited and let it get to the end of the block before he proceeded. He wanted room to move if he had to. The bus turned left off the boulevard, and Somerset picked up speed again. A few minutes later he flipped on his directional to turn onto the ramp that led to the freeway.

As soon as he merged into the flow of traffic on the freeway, Somerset breathed a little easier. Mills let Doe sit up, and he started to hum again, barely audible. Somerset tried to concentrate on the road, but he was having a hard time. Having Doe in the backseat was like having a tick on your back where you couldn't reach it. Somerset couldn't stop glancing back at him in the rearview mirror.

"Who are you, John?" he finally had to ask. "Who are you really?"

The placid expression suddenly sharpened as Doe stared into Somerset's eyes in the mirror. "What do you mean?"

"I mean, at this point, what would it hurt if you told us a little bit about yourself?"

Doe rolled his head on one shoulder, his eyes going out of focus as he thought about it for a moment. "It doesn't matter who I am. Who I am means absolutely nothing." Suddenly he perked up. "You have to take the next exit to get on the highway north."

Somerset put on the directional and merged into the right lane.

"Where we headed?" Mills asked.

"You'll see." Doe was staring intently through the wire mesh at the road ahead.

"We're not just going to pick up two more bodies, are were, Johnny?" Mills said. "That wouldn't be . . . Oh, I don't know, shocking enough. Not for you. Not for the newspapers."

"If you want people to pay attention, Detective, you can't just tap them on the shoulder anymore. You have to hit them over their heads with a sledgehammer. Then you have their *strict* attention."

"So what makes you so special that people should pay attention to you?"

"It's not me. I'm not special. I'm not exceptional at all. *This* is, though. What I'm doing."

"I don't see anything unusual about these precious

murders of yours," Mills said. "As far as I can tell, you're just another run-of-the-mill sicko."

Doe laughed. "That's not true. You know it's not. You're just trying to rile me."

"Johnny, in two months no one's even going to remember this ever happened. There'll be something else in the papers that people will be talking about. Think about it. Something could happen in Washington today that'll knock you right off the front page. By next week, no one's gonna give a shit about you."

Doe closed his eyes and sighed. "Detective, you can't see the whole, the whole complete act. But when this is done, it's going to be so . . . so—"

"Spit it out, Johnny."

"It's going to be *immaculate*. People will barely comprehend it, but they won't be able to deny its magnitude."

Mills shook his head and smirked. "I can't wait."

Doe licked his lips. Suddenly there was desperation in his face. "It is going to be something that will not be forgotten. Never. Believe me, Detective."

"Well, I'll be standing right beside you the whole time, Johnny. You just be sure to let me know when this thing gets started. I don't want to miss any of it."

"Don't worry, Detective. You won't miss a thing."

The voices came through loud and clear through the earplug that California wore under his helmet. Both body mikes were working fine. Down below the freeway stretched out into the distance, like a roll of toilet paper kicked out into the desert. He looked through his binoculars at the metallic-blue sedan a good half mile ahead, then glanced back to the two sharpshooters sitting at the open bay. Their rifles were propped between their legs, muzzles up.

California tapped the pilot on the arm. "Don't get too close," he said into his helmet mike. "If Doe hears the chopper, he may get hinky."

The pilot nodded and eased up on the stick.

Doe was staring at the people in the passing cars. He was getting fidgety, chewing on his bottom lip, like a kid waiting for something special to happen.

"So what's so exciting?" Somerset asked, trying to catch his eye in the rearview mirror.

"We're getting close," he said. "It's not too far from here."

"I've been wondering about something," Mills said. "Maybe you can shed some light on this for me. Do people know when they're insane? Like, when you're in bed at night and you're about to fall asleep, do you ever just stop and say to yourself. 'Man, oh, man, am I ever nuts. I mean, like, I am a complete fucking fruitcake.' Do you ever say that to yourself, Johnny?"

Doe was unruffled. "If you find it more comforting to label me insane, Detective, I won't object."

"Seems like a pretty accurate label to me, Johnny."

"What I am is something I wouldn't expect you to accept. But, of course, I didn't choose this. I was chosen."

"Sure you were."

Somerset cut in. "I don't have any doubt that you believe that you were chosen, John. But you're ignoring one glaring contradiction."

Doe sat forward and frowned, staring into the rearview mirror. "What do you mean, 'contradiction'?"

"Well, if you were indeed chosen—by some higher power, say—your hand was forced. Wouldn't you say that's so?"

Doe was cautious. "Yes . . . perhaps . . ."

"Then isn't it strange that you would take so much pleasure in all this if you were simply an instrument of God?" Somerset stared into Doe's eyes for as long as he could before he had to look at the road. "You enjoyed torturing those people, John. Now that's not really in keeping with a divine mission, is it?"

Doe looked away. His face was red. For the first time since his surrender, he seemed ashamed. "I . . . I doubt that I enjoyed it any more than Detective Mills would enjoy having some time alone with me in a room without any windows." He shifted his gaze to Mills. "Isn't that so, Detective? How happy would it really make you to hurt me with impunity?"

Mills put on a fake pout. "Oh, Johnny, what makes you think I would do that? I like you. I like you a lot."

"*You* wouldn't do that because you know there are consequences. But it's in those eyes of yours, Detective. Nothing wrong with a man taking a little pleasure in his work. Is there, Detective?" Doe shook his head slowly, his eyes boring into Mills's. "I won't deny my personal desire to turn each sin against the sinner. But all I did was take these people's sins to their logical conclusions."

"You killed innocent people to get your rocks off," Mills said. "That's what you did."

"Innocent? Is that supposed to be funny, Detective? Look at the people I killed. An obese man, a disgusting man who could barely stand up he was so fat. If you saw him on the street, you'd point him out to your friends so they could join you in mocking him. If you saw him while you were eating, you wouldn't finish your meal.

"After him I picked a lawyer. And you both must have secretly thanked me for that one, Detectives. Here was a man who dedicated his life to making money by lying with every breath he could muster in order to keep rapists and gangsters and murderers on the streets."

"Murderers?" Mills said. "Look who's talking."

But Doe ignored him. "A woman who—"

"You mean, murderers like you, right?" Mills pressed.

Doe spoke louder to override him. "A woman so ugly on the inside that she couldn't bear to go on living if she couldn't be beautiful on the outside. A lazy drug dealer—a lazy drug-dealing pederast to be accurate." He laughed dismissively. "And let's not forget the disease-spreading whore. Only in a world this putrid could you even try to say these were innocent people and keep a straight face. This is the whole point," Doe shouted. "There is a deadly sin literally festering on every street corner, in every home. And yet we tolerate it. All day long—morning, noon, and night. Well, not anymore. What I am doing is setting the example, and it's going to be puzzled over and studied and followed from now on."

Mills laughed in his face. "Delusions of grandeur, my friend."

"You should be *thanking* me."

"And why is that, Johnny?"

"Because through me, you're going to be remembered. Realize that the only reason I'm here right now is because I wanted to be. You did not catch me. *I* came to *you.*"

Mills scowled. "We would have caught you eventually."

"Oh, really? Biding your time, were you? Toying with me? Is that it? You let five 'innocent' people die while you were waiting for the perfect moment to spring your trap?" Doe leaned into Mills's face. "Tell me what it was that gave me away then. What was the clever piece of evidence you had, the smoking gun that you planned to use against me just before I ruined it for you by walking into the precinct with my hands in the air? Tell me, Detective. I want to know."

"I seem to remember us knocking on *your* door, Johnny."

"And I seem to remember bashing you in the face with a two-by-four, Detective. You're only alive right now because *I* didn't kill you."

"Sit back," Mills ordered.

But Doe didn't budge. "I spared you," he whispered in Mills's face. "Remember that, Detective Mills. Every time you look in the mirror for the rest of your life— or should I say for the rest of what life I've *allowed* you to have."

Mills grabbed the front of his jumpsuit and shoved him back against the seat. "I said, sit back, freak. Sit back!"

They glared at each other for only a second because Doe closed his eyes and started taking deep meditative breaths, calming himself. When he finally opened his eyes again, Somerset was staring at him in the rearview mirror. A smile blossomed on his face. "Don't ask me to pity those people, Detectives. I don't mourn them any more than I mourn the thousands who died in Sodom and Gomorrah."

"You fuck!" Mills shouted. "You really think what you did was God's good work?"

Doe bent his head and pressed his thumb to his forehead until fresh blood seeped through his bandaged fingertip. "The Lord works in mysterious ways, Detective." When Doe picked his head up, there was a red smudge on his forehead. He was smiling like a saint.

TWENTY-FIVE

The sky was streaked with crimson as the helicopter continued north, following a two-lane road that led to a series of faceless industrial parks spread out at the edge of the desert. In the distance to the west, an Amtrak train moved like a worm on the horizon. A hundred yards east of the road, huge electrical towers stood in a line that stretched off to the mountains, like giant robot sentinels awaiting orders. The metallic-blue sedan was about a mile ahead, heading north on the industrial road.

In the cockpit, California shook his head. "There ain't no ambush out here," he said to the pilot through his helmet mike. "There ain't no fucking nothing out here."

The pilot pointed at the electrical towers. "I can't land anywhere near those wires. You know that, don't you?"

"I know," California said. He looked through his binoculars. There were factories at the end of the road. Doe could have accomplices, and they could be waiting there. But if they saw the chopper following the car, they'd get hinky. "Go high," California said. "Way up. Just in case someone's waiting for them up ahead."

The pilot nodded as he maneuvered the stick and brought the chopper up higher.

The chopper abruptly pitched to one side, and California's stomach fluttered as they soared above the electrical towers. The two sharpshooters grabbed the handgrips over the open bay, but otherwise they hardly moved from their positions, rifles between their legs at the ready.

"Stop here," John Doe said. "Right here will be fine."

Somerset touched the brake lightly as he scanned the terrain outside. There was nothing, absolutely nothing but desert. The nearest structure was a long, one-story building at least a hundred yards or more away. "Right here?" Somerset asked.

"Yes. Fine."

Somerset brought the car to a halt, but he hesitated before he cut the engine. When he did, the interior of the car was suddenly silent. A stiff desert wind rocked the car ever so slightly as washes of sand pelted the windshield.

Doe looked at Mills. "Can we get out now, Detective?"

Mills and Somerset were looking at each other in the rearview mirror.

Somerset took another look at the landscape outside, then nodded. "But leave the leg irons on." He passed the handcuff keys to Mills through the wire-mesh barrier.

Mills unlocked the cuffs that held Doe to the wire mesh and the ones that linked the handcuffs on his wrists to the leg irons. He passed the keys back to Somerset, then waited for Somerset to get out and open the back door for them. Doe slid out first, then Mills who immediately had to shield his face to keep his eyes from getting sandblasted. Doe was facing away from the car, chuckling to himself.

"What's so funny?" Mills asked.

Doe pointed with his handcuffed hands. About ten feet off the road, the dried-out carcass of a dead dog lay on its side. What was left of its mangy fur swirled in the wind. "I didn't do that one," Doe said, still chuckling.

"Now what, Johnny?" Mills asked impatiently.

Doe nodded toward the industrial park up the road. "That way."

"Why can't we drive there?" Somerset asked.

Doe's face turned serious. "We're not going that far. We can walk."

Mills and Somerset exchanged glances. It was hard to tell if this was the insane demand of a lunatic or part of some calculated plan. Somerset pointed up the road with his chin, and Mills nodded.

"Come on, Johnny. Let's take a walk." Mills started leading Doe up the road toward the industrial park.

Somerset lagged behind, scanning the sky for the chopper. He couldn't see it, but he didn't expect to. They were supposed to keep their distance, so that Doe wouldn't know they were up there. Somerset knew they could get here fast if necessary, but he couldn't imagine what Doe could have up his sleeve. They were out in the middle of nothing. If anyone even tried to get close to them, the chopper would be on them like a hawk on a field mouse.

"What're you looking for?" Somerset heard Mills saying to Doe.

Doe kept looking back toward the car. "What time is it?" he asked.

"Why do you want to know?" Somerset asked. He looked at his watch. It was just past seven.

"I want to know," Doe insisted. "What time is it?"

"Don't worry about it," Mills said, turning Doe back around. "Just keep leading the way."

Somerset's brow was furrowed as he stared back down the road that had brought them here. What the hell was Doe up to? he wondered.

"It's close," Doe said, looking back over his shoulder. "It's coming!"

Somerset squinted down the road. There was something on the horizon, coming toward them. It was a van. A white van coming this way, dust flying in its wake. "Mills!" he shouted as he took out his gun.

Mills saw the van and immediately pulled his weapon, tightening his grip on Doe.

"Stay with him," Somerset shouted as he started running toward the van to head it off.

"Wait!" Mills yelled.

But Somerset kept going. "No time to discuss it."

Doe started to follow Somerset. "There he goes."

Mills leveled his gun in Doe's face. "Stay."

Static crackled in California's earplug as he tried to make out what Mills and Somerset were saying. The pilot had taken the chopper farther off into the desert to keep from being seen.

"...*delivery van*..." Somerset was saying. "...*south*..."

A sudden blast of high-pitched static made California wince. He pounded his helmet to remedy the problem, but he doubted that it would help. The problem was the high-tension power lines. They were breaking up his signal.

Somerset's voice broke through again. "... *don't know what it is...*"

"Shit!" California cursed as he lost the signal again. Was Somerset calling for them or not? He strained to hear something, anything, but now there was only goddamned static.

Mills kept his gun on Doe as he watched Somerset running up the road. He glanced up at the sky. Where the fuck was California? he thought.

Doe was eerily serene. "It's good we have some time to talk, Detective." He started walking toward Somerset again.

Mills grabbed him by the shoulder. "Get down! On your knees. Down!" He kicked Doe's knees out from behind, forcing him to kneel.

Mills positioned himself behind Doe so that he could keep the gun on him while watching Somerset down the road at the same time.

Doe twisted his head back and looked up at Mills. He was smiling that saintly smile again. "You know, Detective, I envy you."

Somerset was out of breath from running in the heat, but he kept walking toward the white delivery van. It was fifty yards off. He pulled down his tie and opened his shirt collar to expose the mike taped to his chest. "Stop the van!" he said again, praying that California could hear him. "Stop the van!"

But the chopper was no where in sight, and the van wasn't slowing down. Somerset pulled his gun and fired a warning shot into the air. Suddenly the van hit the brakes, tires screeching, wheels sliding on the sandy road. Somerset started running again, his gun trained on the cab of the van. He stopped ten yards away from it, gun in a two-hand grip, muzzle leveled on the windshield. He couldn't see who the driver was because of the glare.

"Get out!" he shouted into wind. "Get out with your hands over your head. Do it now!"

The driver's door opened, and a man slid out, hands high. He was a white guy, average build, thinning hair, trim moustache. He was wearing mirrored sunglasses and a dark brown uniform. "Jesus Christ, man, don't shoot me! What do you want? Just tell me! I'll give you whatever you want."

"Turn around," Somerset ordered. "Hands on your head." He moved closer, gun leveled on the man's back.

"What the hell's going on, man?" The delivery man was scared shitless.

"Who are you? What're you doing out here?"

The man looked over his shoulder. "I ... I'm working. I'm delivering a package."

"To who?"

In the helicopter, California strained to hear what they were saying. "*It's just a package for this guy ... Ah, David something.*"

"*David who?*"

"*Ah, ah ... let me think, let me think ... David ... Mills. David Mills. Detective David Mills.*"

"Motherfucker!" California cursed.

The sharpshooters were leaning toward the cockpit, wanting to know what was going on.

The pilot was looking at California. "You want me to go down?"

"No! Wait for Somerset. He said to wait for his signal, no matter what."

Static faded in and out as California listened for voices in the void.

Somerset kept his gun to the man's head as they walked to the back of the delivery van to get the package. "Slowly," he warned as the man opened the rear doors.

The inside was full of all kinds of boxes, packages, large envelopes.

"It's that one," the man said, pointing to a brown cardboard box up near the cab, "the one with all the tape." The box was about one foot square, completely covered with clear reinforced tape. "This . . . this strange guy tipped me five hundred bucks to bring it out here. He said it had to be here at seven o'clock exactly. I know I'm a little late, but—"

"Get it and put it out here on the ground," Somerset ordered. "Slowly."

"Okay, okay." The delivery man climbed in to get it. He stepped back out and set it down on the pavement, then backed away, hands up over his head.

Somerset glanced down at the box, keeping his gun on the man. There was writing on top, in marker: TO DETECTIVE DAVID MILLS—HANDLE WITH CARE.

"Get down on the ground," Somerset said to the man. "Face down and keep your hands on your head."

The man did as he was told. His bare arms were trembling.

Somerset peeled back his shirt and spoke directly into the body mike as he stared down at the box. "There's a package here. It's from John Doe."

"I don't know what it is, but—"

Static drowned out Somerset's voice again. California pounded on his helmet in frustration. He turned to the pilot.

"Call for the bomb squad. Tell them to hurry."

The pilot nodded. "Should I go down?"

"Wait!" California said. "He hasn't given us the word."

The static faded briefly. Somerset's voice came back. *". . . going to open it . . ."*

Mills squinted into the wind. In the distance, Somerset was dragging the delivery man to his feet, frisking him and checking his wallet. The man started to run then, but it was obvious from Somerset's gestures that he was driving the man off, ordering him to run.

Doe rolled his head on his shoulders under Mills's grip. "I wish I could have been a normal man," he said, "like you. I wish I could have a simple life."

Mills tried to make out what Somerset was doing now. He was down on one knee, leaning over something in the road. "What the fuck is going on?" he mumbled to himself.

The wind was whistling in his ears.

"I sent the delivery guy out on foot," Somerset said out loud, hoping that California was getting his transmission. "Have the guy picked up. He's heading south on the road."

He pulled out his switchblade and flicked it open. "I'm opening the package now." His hand was shaking as he sliced through the tape along the top seams. He pulled the flaps back, ripping the remaining tape. Whatever was inside was well wrapped in bubble-pack paper

Suddenly the sound of rotors overtook the whoosh of the wind. Somerset looked up to see the chopper moving in. "Stay back!" he yelled into the mike. "Stay back! I don't know what it is yet."

The chopper changed directions and started to ascend, then held its position, hovering high in the sky.

Somerset used his knife to cut the tape that was holding the bubble-pack paper around the object inside. He tugged on the paper. The object was heavy. It rolled over as he pulled the bubble-pack out. There was coagulated blood on it. He looked inside.

"Oh, Christ . . ." He fell back onto the pavement, suddenly weak, not wanting to look. But he couldn't keep from looking. "Oh, Christ, no . . ."

He stood up, but his legs were shaky. He stumbled back and held onto the van for support. An image of the yellow school bus and all the kids getting off earlier that afternoon jumped into his brain. He felt like throwing up.

"Oh, Christ, no . . ."

Mills watched Somerset stumbling back from the box in the road. Something was wrong. He grabbed Doe by the shoulder of his jumpsuit. "Get up! Stand up! Let's go!"

Doe struggled to his feet and tried to walk, but he

couldn't move fast enough for Mills in the leg irons. "You've made a good life for yourself, Detective—"

"Just shut up and walk!"

Doe tried to pick up his pace, but he tripped and fell. Mills tightened his grip on the jumpsuit and started to drag him. "Get up, asshole! Walk!"

Somerset swiped the tears from his eyes and the saliva from his mouth. He gulped deep breaths, determined to keep it together. But then he looked up from the box and saw Mills dragging Doe toward him. "Oh, fuck, no . . ." he mumbled. "No . . ."

He pushed off the van with his gun hand and bent his head toward the body mike on his chest as he headed toward Mills and John Doe. "California, listen . . . listen to me. Whatever you do, do not come here. *Do not land!* Stay away. No matter what you hear, or what you see, *do not move it!* Doe has the upper hand."

The helicopter moved off to the west as Somerset mustered his strength, trotting toward Mills and Doe as fast as his legs would take him.

The sun was just a sliver over the mountains, casting long shadows on the desert sands. Mills gritted his teeth and pulled Doe to his feet. Something was wrong. Somerset was forty yards off, running toward them.

"Come on! Move, goddamn it!"

But Doe just stood there watching Somerset, his face perfectly serene. "Here he comes."

"Somerset?" Mills shouted. "What the fuck is going on?"

But Somerset couldn't hear him over the blowing wind.

"I wish I could have lived like you do, Detective," Doe said.

Somerset was thirty yards away now. "Put your gun down, Mills!" he shouted. "Throw it away!"

"What?" Mills let go of Doe and stepped toward Somerset, his gun pointed at the ground.

"Throw down your gun now!" Somerset shouted.

"What are you talking about?" Mills shouted back.

Doe's voice came over Mills's shoulder. "Do you hear me, Detective Mills? I'm trying to tell you how much I admire you and your pretty wife . . . Tracy."

Mills wheeled around to face him. "What did you say?"

Doe was smiling.

Somerset ran up behind Mills, out of breath. "Throw your weapon down, Mills . . . That's an order!"

"Fuck you!" Mills snapped. "You're retired. I don't have to listen to you."

"Listen to me, Mills."

But Mills wasn't listening. He was moving in on Doe, the gun in his hand unconsciously leveled on the killer's chest.

Doe was still smiling. "It's disturbing how easily a member of the press can purchase information from the men in your precinct, Detective."

"David . . . please . . ." Somerset pleaded, struggling to catch his breath.

"I visited your home this morning, detective. You weren't there. I tried to play husband, tried to taste the life of a simple man . . . But it didn't work out. I took a souvenir, though."

Mills's face was contorted in pain and confusion as

he turned to Somerset, pleading with his eyes for some answers.

Somerset held out his hand, tears brimming in his eyes. "Give me the gun," he rasped.

"I took something to remember her by," Doe said. "Her pretty head."

Mills was clutching his stomach, begging Somerset for the truth.

"I took it because I envy your normal life, Detective. It seems that envy is *my* sin."

Mills lunged at Doe, grabbing his shirtfront and jamming the barrel of his gun into Doe's eye socket. "It's not true!" he screamed. "Say it! It's not true—"

Cold metal kissed the back of Mills's neck. It was the barrel of Somerset's automatic. "I can't let you do this, Mills."

"What's in the fucking box, Somerset? *Tell me!*"

Somerset's hand was trembling. Tears streamed from his eyes. He couldn't mouth the words.

"I just told you, Detective," Doe said calmly.

"It's not true!"

"Oh, but it is, Detective."

Somerset gasped. "This is what *he* wants, Mills. Can't you see that?"

"Become vengeance, David," John Doe urged.

"Shut up!" Mills yelled.

"Become *wrath*!"

"Shut your fucking mouth!" Mills pistol-whipped him across the face, knocking him over onto his shoulder.

Doe righted himself slowly, like a turtle, unfazed by the blow. He got back to his knees. Blood was trickling down the side of his face. He lowered his head, ready for martyrdom. "Kill me, Detective."

SEVEN

Mills put the gun to Doe's forehead, gripping it in both hands, his chest heaving, sobbing uncontrollably, furious but unsure. He cocked the hammer.

"He *wants* you to do it," Somerset pleaded, still holding his gun on Mills. "Don't do what *he* wants."

Mills pressed the gun into Doe's forehead, pushing his head back.

"You murder a suspect, Mills, and you throw everything away. I won't let you do that."

"Fuck you!" Mills sobbed. "You won't turn me in. We'll say he tried to run, and I fucking shot him. We'll figure out the details later." He ripped off his bulletproof vest, tore open his shirt, and yanked off the body mike, tossing it into the desert. "No one has to know." He tightened his grip on the trigger.

"They'll hang you out to dry, Mills. They won't care who he is. A cop who kills a suspect who can't defend himself? Forget about it. You'll be finished. You'll do time."

"I don't care!"

"If you're gone, Mills, who's going to fight the fight?"

"Fight the fight for what, Somerset? For what? You're giving up the fight. So don't fucking preach to me when you don't even believe it yourself."

"Don't listen to him," Doe hissed. "Kill me!"

"David! You're wrong," Somerset insisted. "Who will take my place if you're not here? Who?"

"Tracy begged for her life, Detective."

Somerset jammed his gun into Mills's neck. "Drop the gun, David."

"It was truly pitiful, detective. She begged for her own life . . . and for the life of the baby inside her."

245

Mills furrowed his brow in confusion, then the horror dawned on him.

Doe looked shocked. "You didn't know?"

Mills's lips trembled, his hands shaking wildly as he held the gun to the killer's forehead.

A wave of fatigue suddenly descended over Somerset. His arms were so tired he dropped the gun to his side. "If you kill him, David, he wins."

Doe closed his eyes, hands clasped in prayer.

The gun rattled in Mills's shaking hands. "Okay . . . he wins."

The gun went off, and the top of Doe's head flew off as he toppled backward. Bloody chunks littered the dusty road. The report of the gunshot echoed across the desert, then gradually faded, replaced by the whistle of the wind.

Mills dropped his gun to the pavement. He turned and started to walk, but only took a few steps before he fell to his knees and buried his face in his hands.

Somerset stared down at the corpse, his mouth bone-dry. A growing pool of blood from what was left of Doe's head spread out on the pavement, like a bad idea. It seeped under Mills's gun—a dull silver island in a crimson lake. Somerset closed his eyes. He didn't want to see anymore.

Two hours later Somerset was still on that stretch of road, leaning on the fender of the metallic-blue sedan that had brought him there, a cold cup of coffee in his hand. A circle of police cars beamed their headlights onto the crime scene. Doe's corpse was in a black body bag a few feet from the blood-smeared pavement. Two attendants from the medical examiner's office picked up the bag as if it were a heavy piece of luggage, set it on a gurney, and wheeled it to their van. Plainclothes cops and forensics technicians were scattered all around the scene. The helicopter was out in the desert fifty yards off the road, its rotors still. Mills had been whisked away over an hour ago.

Somerset was staring down at the wallpaper rose, thinking.

The captain broke away from a group of detectives and walked over to Somerset. "It's over, William. Go home."

Somerset sighed. "What happens to Mills now?"

The captain shrugged. "He goes on trial. The police union will get him a good lawyer. He won't get the max because of mitigating circumstances, but he'll serve some time. No doubt about that."

"And his career?"

The captain shook his head. "Forget about it."

"So Doe did win. He got seven for seven . . . seven lives destroyed. Eight if you count Mills . . . Nine actually if you count . . . the baby." Somerset had a hard time saying it.

"Go home, William," the captain repeated. "You're retired now. Start putting this behind you."

Somerset shook his head as he crumpled up the wallpaper rose. "I've changed my mind."

"What?"

"I'm staying on. I don't want to retire."

"Are you sure?"

"I'm sure." He got up off the car and walked around to the driver's side. "See you Monday," he said.

As he opened the car door, he tossed the crumpled

piece of wallpaper into the desert where the wind picked it up like a tumbleweed. He knew he could never leave now. With Mills gone, someone had to stay to fight the fight.

He was a charming hitchhiker with a body to die for in *Thelma and Louise*. He was the sensuous undead in *Interview with the Vampire*. And in *Legends of the Fall*, his first big romantic lead, he was simply drop-dead gorgeous. How did a sensitive Missouri boy end up as the male sex symbol of the 1990s?

It's time to get a closer look at the real Brad Pitt— an irresistible mix of hellraiser and choir boy who dropped out of college just two credits short of graduating to head for Hollywood.

Packed with lots of details, and 16 irresistible pages of photos, Chris Nickson's stunning biography is the best way to get into Brad Pitt's world.

Go behind the scenes into the life and career of Hollywood's sexiest hunk

BRAD PITT

CHRIS NICKSON

— Coming in October 1995 —

_____ 95727-0 $4.99 U.S./$5.99 Can.

The SILENCE of the LAMBS

THE ELECTRIFYING BESTSELLER BY
THOMAS HARRIS

" THRILLERS DON'T COME ANY BETTER THAN THIS."
—CLIVE BARKER

"HARRIS IS QUITE SIMPLY THE BEST SUSPENSE NOVELIST WORKING TODAY." —*The Washington Post*

Alcatraz. The prison fortress off the coast of San Francisco. No man had gotten out alive before his time was up, until a 20-year-old petty thief named Willie Moore broke out.

Recaptured, then thrown into a pitch-black hellhole for three agonizing years, Willie is driven to near-madness—and finally to a brutal killing. Now, up on first-degree murder charges, he must wrestle with his nightmares and forge an alliance with Henry Davidson, the embattled lawyer who will risk losing his career and the woman he loves in a desperate bid to save Willie from the gas chamber.

Together, Willie and Henry will dare the most impossible act of all: get Willie off on a savage crime that the system drove him to commit— and put Alcatraz itself on trial.

MURDER
IN THE FIRST

DAN GORDON

NOW A MAJOR MOTION PICTURE STARRING CHRISTIAN SLATER, KEVIN BACON, AND GARY OLDMAN

They were called the class from Hell—thirty-four inner-city sophomores she inherited from a teacher who'd been "pushed over the edge." She was told "those kids have tasted blood. They're dangerous."

But LouAnne Johnson had a different idea. Where the school system saw thirty-four unreachable kids, she saw young men and women with intelligence and dreams. When others gave up on them, she broke the rules to give them the best things a teacher can give— hope and belief in themselves. When statistics showed the chances were they'd never graduate, she fought to beat the odds.

This is her remarkable true story—and theirs.

DANGEROUS MINDS

LOUANNE JOHNSON

NOW A MAJOR MOTION PICTURE FROM HOLLYWOOD PICTURES STARRING

.MICHELLE PFEIFFER